Andrew Puckett was born in Sherborne, Dorset. He has worked in various hospitals in Taunton, London and Oxford, and in the latter city was for many years Microbiologist at the Blood Transfusion Centre. He draws on these experiences for his hospital-based crime novels. He now lives in Taunton with his wife and two daughters.

A LIFE FOR A LIFE

When Dr Fraser Callan claims that Alkovin, the new 'wonder-drug' for leukaemia, has dangerous side effects, his boss, Connie Flint, sends him to America for three months to shut him up. Fraser's previous boss and mentor, Dr John Somersby, has been murdered. Somersby had refused to have anything to do with Alkovin, but following his death, Connie and her colleagues have been persuaded by a pushy drugs rep to begin a medical trial with the drug. Then Fraser returns from America to discover that Frances, his fiancée, has contracted leukaemia and Connie is treating her with Alkovin . . .

Books by Andrew Puckett
Published by The House of Ulverscroft:

TERMINUS

ANDREW PUCKETT

---◆---

A LIFE
FOR A LIFE

Complete and Unabridged

ULVERSCROFT
Leicester

First published in Great Britain in 2000 by
Constable & Robinson Limited
London

First Large Print Edition
published 2002
by arrangement with
Constable & Robinson Limited
London

British Library CIP Data

Puckett, Andrew
A life for a life.—Large print ed.—
Ulverscroft large print series: mystery
1. Jones, Tom (Fictitious character)—Fiction
2. Drugs—Great Britain—Testing—Fiction
3. Suspense fiction
4. Large type books
I. Title
823.9'14 [F]

ISBN 0–7089–4629–1

Published by
F. A. Thorpe (Publishing) Ltd.
Anstey, Leicestershire
Set by Words & Graphics Ltd.
Anstey, Leicestershire
Printed and bound in Great Britain by
T. J. International Ltd., Padstow, Cornwall

This book is printed on acid-free paper

I am grateful to Dr Mary Tyne,
Barry Gray and John Croxton for
their professional help with this book.
Also, as always, to Carol Puckett
for her indispensable assistance
in writing it.

For my mother and her sister Marjorie

1

May 1999

She came in quickly, breathlessly, aware that Sean was looking at the clock on the wall.

'I'm sorry, Sean. I don't know what's the matter with me at the moment . . .'

He smiled at her — because he liked her, because her tardiness was so uncharacteristic. 'All right, Frances.' A thought struck him: 'Perhaps you'd like to be control, then? As a penance.'

She groaned. 'Oh, if that's what it takes . . .'

A minute later, in the cubicle, she winced as he deftly thrust a needle into a vein.

'When's Fraser due back?' he asked as blood flowed into the sample tube. 'This week, isn't it?'

'Friday,' she said, smiling now — to herself as much as him. 'Midnight.'

'Are you meeting him at the airport?'

'Sure am.'

He grinned at her, then took the sample back to the laboratory and gave it to one of the others to put through the analyser. She staunched the bleeding, put a plaster on the wound and went to sign reports in the office.

She had no foreboding until Connie Flint, the department's medical director, phoned through and asked to see her.

Something to do with Fraser? she wondered as she walked down the corridor; her fiancé, who was a registrar in the department, didn't exactly see eye to eye with Connie.

'Sit down, Frances,' Connie said. Then: 'I'm afraid I've got some bad news for you . . . ' She hesitated. 'Sean brought me the count and a film from the blood he took from you and . . . well, it looks like leukaemia . . . '

* * *

Connie was still talking — at least, Frances assumed she was because her lips were still moving. She tried to concentrate.

' . . . hope I'm wrong . . . need to look at some bone marrow . . . suggest we do that now . . . '

'Yes, Dr Flint,' she said, her voice barely above a whisper.

'D'you need a few minutes?'

'No. No, thank you.'

They went along to the treatment room, where a nurse was waiting. Frances slowly stripped to the waist and lay on the bed. She felt as though her doppelgänger was watching

2

her and wasn't sure which of them was which.

Connie drew on sterile rubber gloves. 'You've heard this often enough, but I'll say it again anyway — you shouldn't feel anything other than the aspiration of the fluid.'

Frances nodded, unable to speak.

Connie filled a syringe with local anaesthetic. 'Here we go, then.' Her voice was calm, neutral, but as she looked down at the younger woman's breasts, an emotion akin to hatred flashed through her brain, and as her eyes were drawn up to the calm, alabaster face with its latent beauty and frame of near black hair, she thought, *Even now, you're so bloody cool, aren't you?*

She forced herself to relax as her fingers probed Frances' sternum, then she injected the fluid round the point she'd found and gave it a few moments to work. Then she picked up the cannula and, without hesitating, pushed the point through the flesh until she felt it reach the bone. She took a breath and with a sudden effort, thrust it through into the marrow.

'OK?'

Frances nodded again. She'd felt no pain, only a vague, dull crunch. Connie fitted a syringe to the cannula and eased the plunger up . . .

'*Ahhh!*'

'Sorry, nearly done . . . '

'Not a happy sign though,' Frances managed between her teeth — the pull on the marrow is notably more painful in leukaemia . . .

★ ★ ★

Don't let it be, please don't let it be . . . They were back in Connie's office and Frances wasn't sure who she was addressing the words to, but felt vaguely that it must be God, which seemed strange, since she didn't believe in Him . . . then Connie looked up from the microscope and her expression told her the worst.

'It's ALL,' she said. 'I'm terribly sorry, Frances, but there's no point in my pretending otherwise. Of course, we'll do a FACSCAN to make sure, but I don't think there can be any doubt . . . ' *I'm gabbling,* she thought, *because — because I don't like her* . . . 'Is there anyone you'd like to phone?'

Frances looked up, her grey eyes looking deep into Connie's blue ones. *You're not sorry,* she thought with sudden perception. *You've handed me tantamount to a death sentence and you're not truly sorry. How I wish you were someone else.* She wanted to

4

cry, but couldn't bear to in front of Connie. *If only John Somersby were still alive* . . .

'I'll phone my mother in a minute,' she said, 'but . . . where do we go from here?' As she said it, she realised the word *we* put her completely in Connie's hands.

Connie took a breath. 'I'd like to start treatment straight away, first thing tomorrow morning.'

'Which drugs?'

'Oh, it has to be Alkovin, DAP — I think you know that.'

Frances looked steadily back at her.

'I know what you're thinking, Frances — let me show you something.' She got up and pulled open a filing cabinet. 'Fraser isn't the only one here who can collate figures.' She drew out a folder. 'You know what the cure rate is for acute lymphoblastic leukaemia in adults?'

'Twenty to thirty per cent?'

'Nearer thirty in a woman. Now look at this — using Alkovin on these patients, we've achieved a greater than ninety-five per cent remission. Now, I know the relationship isn't absolute, but the better the remission rate, the better the cure rate.'

She leaned forward, fixed Frances with her gaze. 'I believe that by using Alkovin, we can raise this to forty, even fifty per cent. Are you really going to tell me that you don't want to try that because of Fraser's fears, because of a *theoretical* risk of depression?'

Frances' mind whirled. *She wants to use me to get at Fraser . . . to prove him wrong about Alkovin — by curing me with it.* 'No, Dr Flint,' she said at last.

Connie let out a breath. 'Good,' she said, softly. Then: 'If you do experience depression or any of the side-effects that Fraser *thinks* he's observed, then we'll treat them along with the others.'

★ ★ ★

Later, back at home, she was at last able to cry, in the arms of her mother.

Rocking her, smoothing her brow and murmuring endearments, Mary Templeton thought sadly, *To think I was regretting that my days of mothering were over . . .*

Later still, while she was helping Frances to pack, she said, 'Are you sure about not telling Fraser, dear?'

'Mum, I want to try this treatment, even if there is a slight risk, and I'm afraid that Fraser would try to stop me . . . I want to live, Mum.'

★ ★ ★

Fraser could never decide whether it was better to meet the customs officers' gaze directly (too honest — something to hide) or avoid it altogether and walk past as though they weren't there (too shifty — something to hide). It was ridiculous anyway, he had nothing over the legal allowance, and yet customs always made him feel conspicuous and guilty.

They didn't stop him. They never had, and probably never would, he supposed, until the day came when he really did have something to hide.

He walked through and scanned the faces on the other side of the barrier . . . She wasn't there — then his eyes flicked back to a face that was familiar — Mary, her mother. He waved, walked swiftly round the barrier and over to her.

'Mary, is something wrong?'

'Fraser, I've got some bad news . . . '

He went still. 'What is it, tell me.'

'She's ill, she asked me to meet you — can we find somewhere to sit down?'

The only place nearby was an unwelcoming set of table and chairs in glass and chrome. He took her arm and propelled her over, dragging his case after him.

'What is it?' he said again as they sat.

'She's in hospital . . . ' She hesitated. 'She's got leukaemia.'

She spoke so quietly that he thought he'd misheard and made her say it again: 'She's got leukaemia.'

'Are you sure?' As the words came out, he could feel their fatuousness.

'Of course I'm sure,' she snapped. 'What do you take me for?'

He stared at her open-mouthed. 'But she was fine on Sunday when we spoke on the phone.'

'She's been feeling tired a lot lately, although we had no idea she was so ill . . . ' She told him how the disease had been found by accident in the laboratory.

He closed his eyes for a moment. 'I'm sorry, Mary. I'm just finding it hard to take in. Who's in charge of her? Oh *no*, not Connie . . . ?'

'Yes,' Mary said with a trace of defiance, 'Dr Flint — and she couldn't have been more helpful.'

'Did she say what kind of leukaemia?'

'Yes, acute something . . . '

'Myeloid, or lymphoblastic?'

'That's it — lymphoblastic.'

'Has she started treatment yet?'

'Yes, that's why she went into hospital.'

Fraser let out a groan. 'Did she say what

8

the treatment was?'

'Yes, but I can't remember — '

'Was it Alkovin? DAP?'

'Something like that.'

He brought his fist down on the table. 'Why did she not *tell* me, Mary, *phone* me? I'd have come straight back.'

Mary hesitated again, then said, 'Because she *wanted* to have the treatment Dr Flint offered, she thought it was her best chance.'

Fraser groaned again and sank his head into his hands.

Mary said timidly, 'She told me you didn't approve of it, but Dr Flint convinced her it gave her the best hope. She convinced me too, Fraser.'

He scrambled untidily to his feet. 'I'm goin' to see Frances now, then I'm goin' round to Connie's and have it out with her.'

'Fraser, you *can't*, it's past midnight — '

'I don' care about — '

'*Fraser!*' she snapped, making him jerk. 'Don't be foolish. Let Frances sleep, let me take you home and you can go and see her first thing tomorrow.' Then she said, 'She's my daughter, Fraser, I'm suffering too, you know.'

'Aye, I know that,' he said more calmly, putting his hand on hers. She looked back at him, aware of the Glasgow burr leaching into his speech.

As soon as they were outside, she fumbled in her bag, brought out a pack of cigarettes and lit one. 'Yes, I've started again,' she said, daring him to object.

They walked to the car-park and she summoned the lift.

'How is she feeling?' he asked as they waited for it.

'Tired, although she was that before. Irritable, sick. She'll feel better for seeing you.'

He nodded. She threw the cigarette away as the lift arrived and they stepped in. 'She's determined to beat it and Dr Flint says the will to live can be a very important factor.'

Fraser bit back the retort that bubbled inside him. The lift stopped and they walked over to her car, a battered black Golf. He offered to drive and she gratefully accepted — it had been even more of a strain than she'd anticipated and she wondered for a moment whether it would have been better to have disobeyed Frances and phoned him in America.

As they left the car-park, she lit up again. The smoke caught the back of his throat and he swallowed a cough — it was her car.

He concentrated on driving and she

studied him covertly as the sodium glare of a street lamp illuminated his face, or rather, the beard that covered most of it. He had a strong Celtic nose and deep-set brown eyes beneath a broad forehead and dark, springy hair ... She knew this already, but what did she know about *him*, Fraser Callan, *Doctor* Fraser Callan?

That he was Scottish, had a temper like quicksilver and wanted to marry her daughter, and that was about all. She liked him, but wished she knew more — a lot might depend on his strength in the months ahead.

Once out of the airport, the calmer, analytical side of his nature reasserted itself and he asked her some more questions, which she answered as best she could.

'Are you sure you'll be all right on your own?' she said when they arrived at his house.

He smiled briefly for the first time. 'Are you offering to stay the night with me then, Mary? People might talk, you know.'

She smiled back. Like Frances, her features seemed almost plain — until she smiled. 'Try not to drink too much, Fraser. You're going to need a clear head tomorrow.'

Good advice, he thought as he watched her drive away and then pulled the door shut behind him. Good, but impractical ... The house smelled slightly musty even though it had only been empty for three days.

He caught sight of a picture of Frances on the mantelpiece, dropped his case and picked up the picture, then sank on to the sofa with his head in hands. He couldn't lose her, *mustn't* lose her . . . Abruptly, he got up, went into the kitchen and found a glass. He opened his case and took out the bottle of duty free scotch.

He had no family here, no friends he knew well enough to disturb this late, so he might as well hold a dialogue with Johnnie Walker. The screw top snapped satisfyingly as the metal seal broke and the spirit gurgled into the glass.

Moral cowardice? Maybe, but it wasn't every day you learned that the woman you loved was mortal sick.

He took a long swallow and picked up the picture again . . . She smiled back at him, and for a moment her face seemed to move as though she was trying to tell him some-thing . . .

Why hadn't she phoned him?

Words he'd say when he saw her started going through his head, and then the words he'd say to Connie . . . To stop the treatment now would probably do more harm than good, but he'd fine well have words to say to her, by *God* he would — this was *her* doing, it was as though she was issuing a challenge to him . . .

He tossed off the contents of his glass, then became aware of an urgent need to empty his bladder, and by the time he came back, the whisky fumes had already begun to blur the edges. He refilled the glass and looked at the picture again.

If I'd never come here, if I'd stayed in Scotland, would this have happened?

Of course it would, it's just that he wouldn't have known about it . . .

But *would* it? Had his presence somehow precipitated events? Now, his mind swirled with guilt and uncertainty.

He turned his thoughts back to when they'd first met, smiled as he drank and thought about it . . .

When had it become inevitable that he would come here and press the button marked Go? He pondered this as he drank and refilled his glass, and just before he passed out he saw everything with perfect clarity — the interview and John Somersby; Terry Stroud and the lab; Connie, Ian and Leo — and Alkovin . . .

Alkovin. It was already behind a lot of misery. Had it been behind John Somersby's murder as well . . . ?

2

'Do sit down, Dr Callan.' The man in the middle had waited while Fraser did so, then had continued, 'I'm John Somersby, medical director here, and I'm flanked, so to speak, by my colleagues: Connie Flint — ' a honey-haired woman with an attractive oval face nodded to him — 'and Ian Saunders.'

'Hi,' Saunders, a balding, rather long-faced man, said.

Somersby leaned back and smiled at Fraser. 'So, Dr Callan . . . we've read your application and CV, we know you'd like the registrar's post here and why — so perhaps you could tell us something about yourself.'

He had a domed bald head, bushy eyebrows and a patrician nose, and his smile told Fraser that he hadn't put the appalling question out of laziness, he knew exactly what he was doing and wanted to see how Fraser would handle it.

Fraser decided to take him at his word.

'Well, I grew up in Glasgow and left school at sixteen to work in the local hospital path lab. I did well enough there in my degree to be accepted at medical school . . . '

He spoke, Somersby noted, with what was clearly a Glaswegian accent, but one that had been smoothed down by . . . time? Or more likely, Somersby suspected, by the ruthless application of emery cloth.

He'd gained his medical degree four years later, he told them (with a distinction, he didn't add, although they knew this from his CV), then served his apprenticeship as a house officer in Edinburgh before specialising in pathology. Over the next half-hour, they questioned him about his experience, the work he'd published and the direction he saw his career going.

There was a slight pause, as there is when an interview is about to change gear, then Somersby looked up.

'Most people who decide on a career in medicine do so from the outset, so to speak, and yet you chose to work in a path lab as a scientific officer. Having embarked on that as a career, what made you decide to change to medicine?'

Fraser thought quickly and again decided on the truth.

'The school I went to in Glasgow was of the kind that regards a pupil who becomes a scientific officer as a major academic achievement. Once I was in lab work and studying for a degree, I realised I had a facility for academic study and that I could aim much higher.'

'But what made you choose medicine? You had a first class honours degree, you could have done a PhD and gone into industry — and probably earned more than we do here.'

Fraser took a breath. 'I think it was a fascination with the human body, and also with what I saw going on around me . . . I watched the pathologists at work and realised that that was what I wanted to be — in both medicine and science.'

Somersby nodded and Connie Flint leaned forward.

'Do you regard your experience as a lab worker as an advantage or a disadvantage to your career now?'

'Oh, very much an advantage.'

'Why?'

'I believe it enables me to see both sides of laboratory practice more clearly — the medical and the scientific.'

She smiled at him. 'Are you suggesting that the rest of us here can't?'

Fraser smiled back. In the beam of her ultramarine eyes, he realised she wasn't just attractive, she was beautiful — and sexy. 'No, I'm not suggesting that,' he said, 'although there are some who can't, just as there are some lab workers who can't, or won't, understand the medical point of view.'

'But of course they can't — they're not doctors.'

Careful . . . 'I used the word in the sense of sympathy. I do believe that a little more understanding on both sides would result in more effective pathology.'

'Could you give us an example of that?' Saunders asked.

Somersby was listening attentively to everything and Fraser somehow wasn't surprised when a week later he was offered the post.

*   *   *

The thing Fraser had liked most about working with John Somersby was his manner with his patients. No matter who they were, or what their medical condition, he seemed to have the right word or gesture for them. Once, he sat beside an elderly woman who was unconscious and clearly dying, just holding her hand and looking at her face. After a full minute, he patted her hand before replacing it gently on the bed and ushering them all out.

'She won't last the day,' he said briefly.

'Have you phoned her family?' he asked the ward sister.

'They're on their way.'

'Good.'

Next was Mrs Eva Norton, a schoolteacher aged forty-nine with acute myeloid leukaemia. After several months on drug therapy, she had relapsed and was taking it badly.

'I'm going to die, aren't I, doctor?'

'Well, we all are one day, but — '

'How long have I got? Please be honest with me . . .'

'I was about to say that I hope to keep you on this planet for longer than myself. This relapse is a set-back, but that's all. I'm quite sure that we can get you into remission again, and then we'll go for a marrow transplant.'

'The last ditch, eh, doctor?'

'Not at all,' he said, injecting the words with belief. 'I could name you a dozen people who are alive and well today thanks to a marrow transplant.'

As though she hadn't heard him, she said, 'I keep asking myself what I've done to deserve this. Have I offended God in some way?'

He said gently, 'You know I can't answer that, dear. Would you like me to ask the chaplain to come and see you?'

'Certainly not!' she said, some of her spirit returning. 'That pompous old fool doesn't know what he believes.'

'Would you like me to call your parish priest?'

'Yes, please,' she said in a smaller voice.

Outside, Connie said, 'Isn't it strange how people say 'be honest with me' when they mean the very opposite. How do you rate her chances, John?'

'It depends on whether we can find a compatible donor . . . ten per cent?'

When the ward round was finished, Somersby asked Fraser along to his office. After enquiring how he was settling in, he said, 'I'm going to ask you to take on laboratory liaison for a few months — no, it's not because of your background,' he added at Fraser's smile, 'it's something all our registrars here do. Although, then again,' he continued slowly, 'it *is* partly because of your background.' He met Fraser's eyes. 'I think we may have a problem here with our laboratory.'

'What kind of problem?' Fraser asked.

Over the past few months, he told Fraser, several GPs and consultants had commented to him how the lab seemed to be becoming less helpful in its attitude, doing the bare minimum requested and nothing more.

'Have you spoken to the lab manager about it?'

'No, I haven't, because I want you to look at the situation in the raw, so to speak.'

* * *

Laboratory liaison hadn't been too onerous, mostly dealing with blood films referred to him by the scientific staff or fielding the numerous phone enquiries that needed a medical opinion, so he had plenty of time to try and diagnose the malaise that Somersby felt existed.

The first thing he noticed was how easy and relaxed the atmosphere was when Terry Stroud, the lab manager, wasn't there, and how everything closed up when he was.

And yet there was nothing particularly menacing about Terry; he was smallish, dapper, somewhere in his fifties with thinning sandy hair and inoffensive brown eyes. He'd seemed pleasant and friendly enough when he'd shown Fraser round, although Fraser couldn't help feeling that he didn't really understand some of the things he was supposed to be explaining.

Then, a few days after Fraser had started, Terry came in holding a form.

'Steve?' He went over to where Steve Lovell, who'd recently moved from another lab, was working. 'Did you authorise this?'

Steve looked at it. 'Yes. Is there a problem?'

'There certainly is, you can't just do a Paul Bunnell test when it hasn't been asked for.'

'But there were atypical monocytes in the film, and — '

'Then that's what you should put on the form, and nothing else. You can't do unauthorised tests — it's against the regulations.' He paused. 'Is that clear?'

Steve pressed his lips together, then said, 'Yes.'

'Good.'

Fraser heard all this, also saw Sean Callaghan and the raven-haired girl whose name he didn't know look at each other and raise their eyes to heaven, so as Terry was on his way out he called him into the doctor's room and shut the door.

'I couldn't help overhearing you just now,' he said. 'D'you mind if I take a look at that form a minute?'

Terry obviously did mind, a lot, but he handed it over. Fraser studied it, then said, 'I don't wish to seem controversial, Terry, but it seems to me that Steve was right to do a Paul Bunnell in this case.'

21

'But you know the regulations, Fraser — no test is to be carried out without medical authorisation.'

'Isn't the fact that I'm here medical authorisation?'

'No, I don't think it is — the regulations state that only the patient's GP is authorised to request tests.'

'Ach, come on, Terry, that's the letter of the law as opposed to its spirit. If Steve sent this out with just 'atypical monocytes' written on it, the doctor might have no idea he was dealing with a case of glandular fever. The Paul Bunnell tells him he is.'

Terry swallowed with irritation. 'If he didn't know, then he could phone you and ask.'

'And then he'd have to call the patient back to the surgery, bleed him again and then send the sample to us again — is that a good use of resources?'

'With respect, Fraser, that is not the *point*.' Terry's voice rose an octave as his eyes twisted around. 'The fact is, Steve could be sued for *assault*, that's what testing a patient's blood without authorisation is. I'd have thought that you, as a doctor, would have realised that.'

Fraser stifled a groan. 'Terry,' he said, 'there is no way we would allow Steve to be sued for using his common sense and saving everybody time and money.'

'You can say that, Fraser, but if the GP or the patient decided to sue, it would be out of your hands, wouldn't it? I suggest that you have a look at the regulations.'

★ ★ ★

'The problem is Terry Stroud,' he told Somersby a week later and explained why.

'I don't think he's being deliberately malicious,' he said. 'I've talked to Sean and he says that Terry's been getting more and more like this over the last year. He's out of his depth, he can't keep up with the technology, and it's made him feel inadequate, so he uses the rules and regulations to try and assert his authority. Maybe he can't help it, but he's the problem.'

Somersby sighed. 'I wondered if it was something like that. The thing is, Fraser, what can we do about it?'

'Early retirement? He's fifty-seven — I checked.'

'There are two problems there: one, he's made it plain he doesn't want to go; secondly, early retirement costs money and the Trust tries to avoid it unless there's a very good reason.'

'The standard of patient care is a pretty good reason.'

'You really think it's that serious?'

'Aye, John, I do.'

Somersby nodded to himself. 'Then we'll have to see what can be done.'

The following week, he called a meeting of the department's medical staff.

'We have two items to discuss,' he said. 'We'll start with Parc-Reed's offer, since I'm sure Mr Farleigh's time is as valuable to him as ours is to us.' He smiled at the company rep seated at the far end of the table. 'Over to you, Mr Farleigh.'

'Thank you, Dr Somersby.' Leo Farleigh opened his briefcase and took out some glossy sheets. 'I'll start by passing these round for you to study.'

He was the archetypal rep, Fraser thought: very smartly dressed, every hair in its place, his square-jawed face closely shaved.

'Has everyone got one? Good . . . ' The macho black moustache must be to compensate for his lack of inches . . . 'Parc-Reed are about to launch a new leukaemia drug in the UK. You may have heard of it — Alkovin.' He looked round at their faces — Somersby, Connie, Ian Saunders, Fraser, and the department's two SHO's, Mark and Sophie.

'It's a Vinca alkaloid, but with a completely

24

new synthetic component. We've trialed it in the States and, in a combination with Daunorubicin and Prednisolone which we call DAP, it shows a remission rate of ninety-five per cent.'

'Golly,' said Sophie, who sometimes sounded as though she hadn't left school.

'Golly indeed,' said Ian Saunders. 'I think we'd all agree that that represents a major step forward.'

Leo went on to tell them that the company now planned a trial in the UK and thought that Avon might be interested.

'We're offering you not only the opportunity to get in on the ground floor — there's no doubt you could get a major paper out of this — but also preferential charges when Alkovin goes on to the market.'

Prompted by Ian and Connie, he described the administration, dosage and contraindications of the drug.

'What about side-effects?' asked Somersby, who hadn't spoken much until now.

'Pretty much as you'd expect — nausea and vomiting, hair loss, some tissue necrosis on extravasation.'

'What about neurological and psychotic effects?'

'There is some neuropathy, as there is with all — '

'That wasn't what I asked,' Somersby interrupted.

'Perhaps I'd better explain,' he said, looking round. 'I've had a report of severe psychosis with this drug.'

'May I enquire from where?' Leo asked, suddenly alert.

'A colleague in America. He's observed depression, delusions and paranoia in a number of his patients.'

'Depression can't be uncommon in leukaemia patients, surely?'

'This was clinical, as were the other symptoms.'

'I assume this was in combination with Prednisolone?'

'Yes.'

'A drug that's known to have neurological effects.'

'Indeed, but not to this extent.'

There was a short pause, then Connie said, 'Can you check this out from your end, Leo?'

'I'd be glad to. It would help if I could have the name of your source, Dr Somersby . . . '

Somersby shook his head. 'That's confidential, Mr Farleigh. But do check what I've said with your American colleagues. I'd be most interested in their reply. Meanwhile I'll have another talk with my colleague . . . and

26

perhaps we could meet again in a couple of weeks?'

Ian looked as though he was about to say something, but a look from Connie stopped him.

Leo said, 'Well, thank you for your time, Dr Somersby. I'll come back to you when I know more.' A perceptible tightness in his voice betrayed the fact that he'd been expecting more from the meeting.

After he'd gone, Connie said, 'Would you tell us who your source is, John?'

'He specifically asked me not to, so I think I'd better respect that. Sorry.'

Ian said, 'How much credence do you give it, John? I mean, Leo has a point about leukaemics tending to be depressed.'

'Enough credence to make me want to know more before using it here.'

'OK, John, I accept that, but ninety-five per cent . . . it's a breakthrough . . . I think most of our patients would jump at it, depression or no.'

'I take it you hadn't heard about these side-effects?'

'Of course not.'

Somersby nodded. 'Then I wonder whether Mr Farleigh has been a shade less than ingenuous with us.'

'Oh, surely not — ' Connie began, but

Somersby overrode her:

'I think we'll leave it there for now. I'll have another talk with my colleague and we'll see what Mr Farleigh comes up with. The other item I want to discuss,' he continued, 'is the laboratory ... ' He explained how he'd become worried by the recent grumbles about the lab.

'I think we've all been aware of it,' said Ian, 'but to be honest, I think it's a fact of life, something we have to put up with.'

'Can I say something?' Mark asked tentatively.

'Of course,' Somersby said.

'With all due respect to Dr Saunders, I think it's worse than that. Some of the housemen and ward sisters have been telling me how unhelpful the lab's become lately.'

'Then why don't they put in a complaint?' Ian enquired, less than impressed by Mark's due respect.

'They say it's never quite bad enough for that.'

'Well, then — '

'The fact is,' Somersby interposed, 'I asked Fraser to look into it discreetly. Perhaps you'd like to share your observations with us, Fraser.'

Fraser repeated what he'd told Somersby earlier. There was a slight pause when he

28

finished, then Connie said, 'I'm sorry to sound cynical, but couldn't Sean's comments be down to the fact that he wants Terry's job?'

'That wasn't my impression,' Fraser said.

Connie shrugged. 'All right, I accept that Terry can be difficult, but I tend to agree with Ian — that he's a cross we have to bear. For the moment, anyway.'

'But it isn't us that does the bearing, Connie,' said Somersby. 'It's the GPs, the staff on the wards and in the lab and, ultimately, the patients.'

They talked round it, but hadn't reached any conclusion by the time they had to break up for the clinic.

'You feel quite strongly about this, don't you, John?' Connie observed as they got up to go.

'I do, yes. I think he should be retired.'

'Well, we'd all better give it some serious thought, then.'

Fraser had wondered at the time whether there had been a note of calculation in her voice, and a fortnight later, when Somersby turned down Parc-Reed's offer, Connie and Ian raised so many objections to the retirement of Terry that the idea was dropped.

However, in the weeks that followed, Terry

moderated his behaviour slightly, but at the same time favoured Fraser with looks so malevolent as to suggest he knew what Fraser and Somersby had been planning for him.

3

May 1999

He woke on the sofa parched and cramped at around four, drank some water and stumbled into bed. It was probably this that saved him from a worse hangover than the just-about bearable one he had when he woke in the morning.

He showered, washed some paracetamols down with coffee, then backed his MG out of the garage and drove to the hospital.

As he walked to the main entrance, a blackbird sang from a tree whose leaves were so green they seemed to fluoresce, and he was taken by a feeling of such profound surreality that he had to sit down on one of the red metal seats by the main door before his legs gave way.

I'm Fraser Callan, he told himself. *I'm Fraser Callan and I've come to see my fiancée* ... He began taking slow, deep breaths.

'Are you all right, dear?' said an old lady with a Zimmer frame.

'I'm fine,' he said. 'But thank you for your concern.'

'Seeing someone?'

'Yes.'

'Then you'd better have these, they're no use to me.' She tossed him a bunch of flowers wrapped in cellophane and stumped on her way without any further explanation.

He made his way up to the ward and found the sister.

'She's expecting you,' she said. 'Before I take you in, you know she's under reverse barrier?'

'Yes.'

'I know you've just come back from America, have you had any infections — '

'No, sister.'

' — no matter how trivial?'

'No, sister.'

'Even a cold — '

'No, sister.'

'I suppose it's no use asking you not to touch her?'

'Not one whit, sister.'

Filtered air hissed as she pushed open the door.

Frances was sitting up in bed with a magazine she obviously hadn't been reading.

'Hello, Fraser. You look terrible, were you drinking last night?'

'I'll leave you,' said the sister.

'And you look beautiful,' he said, going over to her.

'No I don't.'

But as he said it, he realised it was true; she'd had her hair cut short in an attempt to delay losing it, and the drugs had somehow heightened her normally pale colouring, so that her cheekbones stood out like those of a girl in a Pre-Raphaelite painting.

'I've got some flowers,' he said, holding them up.

'They're lovely . . . '

'An old woman gave them to me.'

'Ever the Scotsman . . . Aren't you going to kiss me?'

He put his hands on her shoulders, feeling the warmth of her; their lips touched, brushing gently, and he wished he could distil the moment . . .

'I can taste the whisky,' she said at last, shakily. 'Did you drink the whole bottle?'

'About half. I couldn't sleep, I was that worried.'

'Oh Fraser, I've been so scared,' she said, her fingers digging into his shoulders. 'Better now. You're not angry with me, are you?'

'Why did you no' tell me? I'd have come straight — '

'I know. I didn't want you to.'

'But *why?*'

She looked down for a moment, then up into his eyes. 'I know how you feel about Alkovin and Connie, but don't you see? This is how she wants to get back at you — by curing me and proving you wrong. She's the best friend we've got, Fraser.'

He didn't say anything. There was no point.

'Hey,' she said, 'it's me, remember? I'm not going to get depressed or paranoid, not now that you're here . . . '

★ ★ ★

Since it was Saturday, the department was almost empty. Fraser raised a hand in reply when someone called out to him, then made his way down the corridor to Connie's room. The door was open.

'Fraser! Come and sit down.' If he hadn't known better, he'd have sworn she was pleased to see him. 'When did you get back?'

'Late last night,' he said as he sat. 'Very late.'

She said, 'You know about Frances?'

'I've just been over to see her.'

'I'm terribly sorry, Fraser. We all are. You know we'll all do our best for her.'

He nodded, unable for a moment to speak. She called up Frances' file on the computer

34

and showed him the results of all the tests they'd done so far.

'She's young and she's healthy, Fraser — I honestly think we've got a good chance of a cure.'

He looked at her face; it was a smooth, impermeable mask, showing proper concern and sympathy, but no clue as to what was going on behind it, no opening for what he had to say.

'I wasn't very happy to find you'd put her on DAP,' he said. 'I'd have liked to be consulted.'

'That was out of my hands, Fraser. I did ask whether there was anyone she wanted to phone, and she said her mother.'

'Nevertheless . . . '

'Nevertheless what?'

'I think I should have been consulted.' He tried to keep his voice calm.

'It's not as though you're her husband, Fraser — besides, I'm not sure I'd have been under any obligation to contact you even if you had been.'

'You know how I — ' he began, but she overrode him.

'So far as I and this department are concerned, DAP is the drug combination of choice. Neither Frances nor her mother made any objection when I explained this to them.

Really, Fraser, I'd hoped you'd come back with a more positive attitude.'

'I have, Connie. While I was in America, I did some research and found John Somersby's original source.' He leaned forward. 'He's assembled more data now and is about to go public with it. Alkovin is a dangerous drug, Connie.'

'Can you give this mysterious source a name?'

'Yes. Dr Sam Weisman, haematologist at Stanford General Hospital, New York.'

Her expression didn't change. 'Have you seen this data for yourself?'

He took an envelope from his pocket and handed it to her. 'I made a copy.'

She extracted some sheets of paper, unfolded them and put on her glasses . . . and he found himself thinking, *She's looking older — is it the glasses, or the stigma of being in charge . . . ?*

She quickly scanned the paper, then went through it again more thoroughly before looking up.

'I'd need more than this to convince me,' she said. 'I haven't noticed anything like this level of disturbance in my patients.'

'Why don't you phone him?'

'I think I will.'

'You notice his findings are in accord with

36

my own observations? In that the effects often don't manifest themselves until after consolidation.'

'Your own observations, as you term them, were based on an insignificant number of patients.'

'But that — ' he indicated the sheets of paper — '*is* a significant number.'

She regarded him in silence for a moment before saying, 'This isn't really getting us anywhere, is it? Will it satisfy you if I speak to Dr Weisman myself and then raise the matter with Parc-Reed again?'

'It'd make me happier, certainly, but there's still the question of Frances.'

'We'll keep a look-out for any signs of depression or any other neurological disturbance, and if they should appear, we'll treat her with antidepressants.'

'By which time it could be too late.'

'Too late for what?'

'The disturbances Dr Weisman describes are profound and can make permanent changes — '

'What are you suggesting then, that we stop the treatment?' Her voice became shrill as her patience gave out.

'No, that would probably do more harm than good at this stage.'

'I'm glad you realise that at least . . . '

'Dr Weisman suggests prophylactic antidepressants, preferably Prozac.'

'I don't see any sign of that here . . . ' She scanned the sheets again.

'Those are his observations. If you look — '

'I'm not happy about prescribing antidepressants without a good clinical reason. Perhaps some counselling would help.'

'If you'll just speak to him on the phone, he'll — '

'Certainly I'll speak to him, but I'm not prescribing antidepressants just on his say-so.'

He gazed back at her, felt his own control slipping . . . 'Tha' is the most blinkered, obdurate piece of — '

'I think you'd better leave, Fraser, before you say something you regret.'

He got slowly to his feet, his pulse dancing wildly in his temples. 'I'm sayin' this, I'm holdin' you personally responsible if anythin' happens to her — '

'Are you threatening me, Fraser?'

'If you care to put it like that, yes, Connie, I am threatening you.'

She laughed, a wild, unpleasant sound. 'With what? What could you possibly do to me?'

He gazed back at her impotently.

'There's nothing, is there, Fraser? Only violence. Dig deep inside yourself and that's the only answer you can find, isn't it?' She leaned forward, spoke softly, almost conspiringly. 'So what are you threatening me with, Fraser? A beating? Or are you threatening to kill me?'

'If anything happened to Frances because of your stupidity,' he said slowly, finding his voice at last, 'I believe I would . . . '

Now she smiled, her eyes flicked over his shoulder and he turned to see Terry Stroud in the doorway staring at them.

* * *

What the hell am I going to do . . . ?

As though by way of answer, the small flock of sparrows that had gathered round him when he'd sat down in the scruffy little park flew off in disgust at his meanness.

The answer, in normal circumstances, would be to come to some sort of accommodation with Connie, even if it meant apologising to her — after all, she was his boss, and his career depended on her blessing. But now, even the most abject of apologies was not going to persuade her to change her mind about treating Frances with antidepressants.

How serious was it? He searched his memory banks for the words Sam Weisman had used . . . 'There's a better than evens chance of getting through the treatment without any symptoms at all . . . ' But for the rest that did have symptoms, there was no way of predicting how serious they would be, or whether the damage they caused would be permanent.

His best chance was to phone Weisman himself before Connie did, explain the situation and hope *he* could persuade her to change her mind . . . He looked at his watch — ten thirty. Was that all? Which meant it would be 5.30 a.m. in New York . . . He'd try him at half-past two.

He leaned back on the tired old bench . . . How had things gotten (he'd been going native) so bad between him and Connie?

Then he smiled with one side of his mouth as the answer, part of it, anyway, came back to him: the conference in Birmingham they'd gone to together almost exactly two years before . . .

4

(i)

May 1997

They'd driven up in her car and the heavy traffic had prevented them talking in anything other than desultory snatches. But as he'd reflected at the time, although she'd always been pleasant and helpful to him, she'd always maintained a certain distance. They'd checked in at the hotel and arranged to meet in the bar in an hour.

He'd unpacked, showered and gone down after fifty minutes so that she wouldn't be left on her own, only to find her already ensconced with a party of others she obviously knew. She introduced him and one of them bought him a drink, but they all seemed to be senior consultants and he quickly found himself out of place.

Nothing overt was said or done, but he realised that staying with them would call for some fairly strenuous shoe-horning on his part, so he finished his drink and quietly slipped away.

He'd grown used to his own company over

41

the years, so he went to the inaugural session on his own. At dinner he ran into some old lab colleagues from Glasgow and spent the evening with them.

He didn't see Connie again until the last evening. He was checking something with the receptionist when she hurried into the foyer, looked round and then said, 'Damn!'

'Problems?' he asked her.

'Oh, hello, Fraser. No, not really. I was going to meet some friends here, but they've obviously already gone.' She smiled. 'My own fault, I told them to go if I wasn't here.'

'You could probably catch them in a taxi.'

But she wasn't entirely sure where they'd gone, she told him, and she certainly wasn't about to chase round Birmingham in a taxi looking for them. She wrinkled her nose rather attractively as she said this. 'What are you doing this evening?' she asked.

'I was about to go over to the Trade Fair. First chance I've had.'

'D'you mind if I come with you?'

'Of course not.'

It was only about a quarter of a mile away, so they walked.

Had he enjoyed the conference? she asked.

Very much, he told her. He'd found the

sessions on tissue typing particularly interesting. 'Did you go?' he asked. 'I didn't notice you.'

'No,' she said, then, after a pause, 'I'm afraid I've rather neglected you.'

'That's all right.' He smiled at her. 'I ran into some old friends from Glasgow.' *I'm quite capable of looking after myself, thank you, ma'am* . . .

She smiled back. 'Good.' *I can see you are* . . .

They pottered round the Trade Fair for half an hour without seeing much to arouse their interest. Fraser's Glaswegian colleagues waved from across the floor.

'Don't let me keep you from your friends,' she said.

'I won't,' he replied.

Ten minutes later, they'd seen enough.

'Where were you going to eat?' she asked.

'I hadn't really thought about it. Back at the hotel, I suppose.'

'Let me stand you dinner,' she said. 'My treat. To make up for my bad manners.'

'You don't have to make up for anything,' he said. 'But I'd be delighted anyway.'

She chose a Mexican restaurant and the hot, spicy food, the cold, heady wine and the mournful voice of the floor singer worked on their reserve and melted it.

'You *are* ambitious,' she said.

He'd just told her how he was prepared go anywhere to make the next jump up the rickety ladder.

'I've no choice,' he said.

'How d'you mean?' she asked, curious.

He thought for a moment, then said, 'With my background, I have to keep going up, I can't afford to mark time.'

He drank some wine as he tried to find the right words.

'It's not just ambition,' he said, 'it's also that I don't really belong anywhere now.' He smiled at her. 'I was as much out of place with my old colleagues as I was with yours . . . so I have to keep going up.'

'I see what you mean,' she said. 'I think — '

'What about you?' he said, anxious to change the subject. 'D'you have any wild beasts to slay?'

'What an interesting turn of phrase.'

He shrugged. 'Sorry.'

'No, I mean it . . . Can I have some more wine, please?'

He topped up her glass and she took a mouthful. 'A year ago, I wouldn't have had the remotest idea of what you were talking about. I might as well admit it, life had been a smooth progression for me until then . . . ' As she spoke, she dipped her finger into the wine

44

and ran it round the rim of her glass. 'I don't know how much gossip you've picked up round the department . . . I know that I'm more than good enough for the job I do, but I won't pretend that having a surgeon for a husband has hindered my career.'

'I don't doubt it,' said Fraser.

'Don't doubt what, that I'm good enough for my job, or that — '

'That you're more than good enough for your job.'

'But you know what they say about surgeons?'

'They say a lot of things about surgeons, Connie. Which had you in mind?'

'Perhaps you should have been a diplomat, Fraser, not a doctor. That without exception they're complete and utter bastards.'

He'd been expecting something more subtle, less obviously emotional.

'Oh, don't worry,' she said, 'I'm not about to embarrass you. It's common knowledge that he ran off with a nurse half his age six months ago.'

'I'm very sorry to hear it.'

Her eyes flicked up. 'You didn't know?'

'I'd heard something. How long had you been married?'

'Seventeen years.'

'Children?'

'Two. Both at boarding school, thank goodness — it meant they missed the worst of the nastiness. Anyway,' she hurried on, 'we were talking about slaying wild beasts . . . I want to rebuild my career.'

'Most people would think that being a consultant haematologist represented a pretty sound edifice,' Fraser said after a pause.

'Yes, but there are those who think that I only got the job because of Charles. That's the beast I want to slay.'

'I thought you said he was a bastard. Rather than a beast,' he added at her puzzled look.

'Oh, I see,' she said, laughing. 'No . . . ' After a pause, she said slowly, 'I won't deny there was a time when it would have been pleasant to see him turning slowly on a spit, but . . . that's in the past, I've moved on from that. I want to put the department on the map, to see us in the forefront . . . ' She giggled. 'Mixing metaphors, always a bad sign. But that's why I was so . . . disappointed when JS turned down the Alkovin trial.'

'I suppose he must have had his reasons.'

'I suppose he must . . . but a ninety-five per cent remission rate — it's revolutionary. I think Leo was right, we could have got a major paper out of it.'

Fraser nodded. 'My instinct would have

46

been to go for it, too. How did you find out about it?'

'Ian and I went to a one-day meeting and Leo buttonholed us about it.'

'What made him choose you? I didn't mean . . . '

'It's all right — Parc-Reed are more or less on our doorstep and we've always had a good relationship with them, and Avon's a big town, a good test bed.'

'Did you ever get to the bottom of the business about the side-effects?'

'Not really. Leo said they hadn't come across anything out of the ordinary in the States, while JS's mysterious friend continued to insist that he had.'

They talked around it a while longer, then Connie paid the bill and they walked back to the hotel. The insistent throb of a disco enveloped them as soon as they walked in.

'There'll be no sleep till this finishes,' Fraser grumbled.

'Oh, don't be such a sourpuss. Come on, it probably finishes at midnight.' She took his sleeve and he allowed himself to be dragged on to the dance floor.

His reluctance wasn't all feigned; he'd never been a very good dancer, even when he'd prowled the clubs in search of girls in his youth. Connie, however, was — and after a while, Fraser forgot his own lack of grace in admiration of hers. He knew she was thirty-nine, eight years his senior, yet her body, inside her thin summer dress, in the stuttering strobe lights, lost twenty of them.

He genuinely had no prescience until a slow record came on and they slipped into a loose embrace, but then he knew beyond doubt.

Pheromones, he thought with part of his mind. *Do I really want this?* he wondered, although his body had already made his mind up for him.

'No, yours,' she murmured when he offered to see her to her room, and he knew she wanted to keep control — *she* would be the one who decided when to part.

The door snicked shut behind him and the kiss was seismic . . . He'd forgotten how a kiss can rock you sideways; he was aware of every part of her body at the same time — her mouth, her tongue, her nipples on his chest through the thin dress, her vertebrae beneath his fingers and the glorious curve of her bum . . .

He kissed her neck, her shoulders, popped the buttons of her dress which she shrugged to the floor, nuzzled her breasts, greedily sucking the swollen nipples into his mouth

. . . They were like puppets, their movements pre-ordained.

Bed, and she groaned softly as he eased his way inside her, then again as she climaxed.

They lay awhile in sweaty post-coital regret, then they did it again.

Later, she propped herself up, looked down into his face.

'That was beautiful, Fraser.'

'Yes.'

'But it didn't happen.'

'No.'

She quickly dressed and left.

And when they'd driven back the next morning, she'd chatted more freely than on the way up, but had never once made recognisance of what had happened.

(ii)

Three months later, John Somersby was thinking about beer and its beneficent effect on mankind. The best thing of all about it, he decided as he walked home, was its levelling effect. Not up or down, he thought, just levelling — he was a convivial man and had just spent a convivial couple of hours playing skittles in the Rising Sun.

He sensed the lights of the car coming behind him at the same time as he heard its engine and stepped to the side of the narrow lane to let it pass. It slowed down and dipped its lights when the driver saw him, but then, to his astonishment, it accelerated and drove straight at him. He tried to jump out of the way, but it hit him a glancing blow on the legs. He was knocked into the steep bank and rebounded into the road.

He felt no pain and was dimly aware that the car had stopped and was reversing. It somehow came as no surprise when, instead of stopping beside him, it quite deliberately ran him over.

His wife, Barbara, phoned the pub at just before midnight, knowing they occasionally let customers stay late, but was told that John had left at just after eleven. She found a torch and set off to look for him. She had been a nurse and knew as soon as she saw him that he was dead; nevertheless, she felt for his pulse, then touched his cheek gently before getting slowly to her feet. It was only when she became aware that she was running that she realised it couldn't help him. She didn't stop, though.

She was interviewed at home by a dark-haired and petite inspector called Lyn Harvey, while other police sealed off the area round the body and the surgeon pronounced him dead. Then the Scene of Crime team got to work, taking photographs and samples.

The pathologist arrived and examined the body. He took his time, but all he would say was: 'I'll tell you more when I do the PM.'

Thus, it wasn't until the next day that the police realised they were dealing with murder.

'He was hit here,' the pathologist said, indicating, 'and the blow broke his left leg, but didn't kill him. He would have been thrown against the bank and fallen back into the road. Then, the car reversed back over him, then forward over him again, and it was this that killed him.'

His pelvis and most of his ribs had been broken and his liver and spleen were ruptured.

'So he would have survived the first injury?' Lyn Harvey asked.

'Almost certainly.'

'Any chance that the rest could have been accidental?'

The pathologist snorted. 'That's your department, but I'd think it was pretty unlikely, wouldn't you?'

The only thing he could add was that he thought the car had a low ground clearance, such as found in a sports car.

The case was handed over to Superintendent Garrett of Criminal Investigations. The first thing he did was to interview Barbara

Somersby again. Their house (hers now) was a pretty cottage a little way off the road and their married daughter had come to stay with her.

'I'm very sorry to have to trouble you at this time,' Garrett said. He was a big man in his forties with no spare flesh, a gingery moustache and widely spaced blue eyes.

'It's all right, I understand,' she said.

You don't, Garrett thought, *yet* . . . Lyn Harvey was there with him.

'I have more bad news for you, I'm afraid,' he said.

She stiffened and her brow creased as she wondered what more there could possibly be.

'There's a possibility, a strong possibility, that your husband was killed deliberately, murdered.'

Her mouth opened, then contracted to a tiny O before she closed her eyes and silently began crying again. Her daughter put her arms around her shoulders, then looked up.

'Are you sure, Superintendent?'

'Not absolutely, no, but it is, as I said, a very strong possibility.'

'But my father didn't have any enemies . . . there was no one who would have wanted to . . . ' She tailed off.

'That's what I need to ask your mother about, anyone with a personal grudge . . . and of course anyone who stands to gain by his death. Anything, no matter how tenuous.'

Barbara Somersby had regained control of herself and wiped her eyes. 'The only person who stands to gain financially is myself, Superintendent,' she said. Her fair hair was going grey and her blue eyes were faded, but the strong bone structure of her face gave it a dignity that Garrett would have sworn was genuine.

'That wasn't what I had in mind, madam.' *Necessarily* . . . 'Did anyone have a grudge against him where he worked?'

She thought about this and he waited. At last:

'You said, no matter how tenuous . . . ?'

He nodded. 'I did.'

'The only thing I can think of, and it *is* tenuous, is a dispute he had with his colleagues a few months ago.'

She told him about Ian and Connie, Parc-Reed and Alkovin. 'But I must emphasise, Superintendent, that it was a professional disagreement between colleagues and I'm sure that Dr Saunders and Dr Flint had accepted the situation.'

'Your husband was their superior?'

'Yes, in effect.'

'And his decision was final?'

'Yes.'

Garrett discreetly nibbled his thumbnail a moment. 'Are either of them likely to . . . take over from your husband?'

'Ian Saunders might, although they could just as easily appoint someone from outside.'

'Not Dr Flint?'

'It's possible, although less likely. She's a woman, Superintendent.'

'I didn't think that was a barrier in medicine.'

'Not perhaps quite as much as in your profession, no.'

He couldn't help glancing quickly at Lyn, whose expression remained studiously neutral.

'So,' he said, summing up, 'Mr Leo Farleigh of Parc-Reed made the initial approach to Drs Saunders and Flint, they tried to persuade your husband to give the drug a trial, but he'd heard rumours that it had side-effects and refused?'

'Yes. He was always very cautious where new drugs were concerned. He could remember Thalidomide, you see.'

He asked her whether Somersby had been regular in the days he had gone to the pub.

'He usually went on Friday, but not Monday as a rule.'

'So why this Monday?'

'He was asked to fill in for someone in a

skittles match.' She smiled, sadly. 'He enjoyed simple pleasures, Superintendent.'

'When was this, Mrs Somersby? When did he know he was going to play skittles on Monday?'

She made a mouth. 'Sunday evening, I think — yes, I'm sure it was.'

'Did any of his colleagues know?'

'I don't think — wait . . . He did tell me that Ian Saunders had wanted to swap on-call with him . . . '

* * *

'Good Lord!' was Ian's reaction when Garrett told him Somersby might have been murdered. 'But he didn't have any enemies . . . '

They were in Garrett's office at the police station. 'You mean, none that you know of, sir,' Garrett said.

Ian shrugged and smiled. 'I suppose that's right.'

When had he last seen him? Garrett asked. — When he left the lab on the afternoon of his death.

Had he seemed worried about anything? — No.

'Did you get on well with him, sir?'

'Yes, very well.'

'I believe there was a dispute concerning a

drug trial a little while ago? Alkovin, produced by Parc-Reed Pharmaceuticals.'

'Oh, that. Hardly a dispute, Superintendent. A minor professional disagreement.'

'Tell me about it.'

'There isn't much to tell . . . '

Garrett and Lyn Harvey listened while Ian explained how Leo Farleigh had approached him and Connie, then how they'd unsuccessfully tried to sell the idea to Somersby.

'So the initial approach was made to you, Dr Saunders?'

'To myself and Dr Flint, yes.'

'Why was that, d'you think? I mean, why approach you and not the person in charge?'

Saunders smiled again — he smiled rather a lot, Garrett noticed. 'John was known for being rather . . . conservative when it came to drugs. Leo thought we'd have a better chance of persuading him between us.'

'But it didn't work out that way?'

'No, it didn't,' Ian agreed.

'Do you still regret that? The decision not to give Alkovin a trial?'

'I do, as it happens. I think the drug has a lot of potential.'

Garrett nodded gently. 'What were you doing last night, Dr Saunders?'

'Last night?'

'Yes.'

Ian looked him in the eye, said lightly, 'Why ask me? Am I a suspect, Superintendent?'

'For elimination purposes, sir. We'll be asking all other parties the same questions.'

Ian nodded slowly, said, 'I was on call.'

'So where would you have been, sir?'

'At home, most of the time. But I was called in, once.'

What time would that have been? Garrett asked. — About half-past nine, Ian thought . . . 'It was a Thrombocytopenia and the platelet count was so low that I thought I'd better come in.'

He'd arrived at the lab at about ten to ten, looked at the film, checked that the appropriate blood products were being prepared and then gone to see the patient. 'After that, I looked in at the lab again and then went home.'

What time had he arrived home? — About half-past eleven.

'Are there any witnesses to any of this, sir?'

'Yes. Steve Lovell, the SO who called me in, will remember me in the lab, the sister on Malvern Ward ought to remember me coming to see the patient.' He smiled again. 'And my wife will remember me coming home.'

'Did you know that Dr Somersby was playing skittles that night?'

Ian blinked at the change of direction. 'I did, as a matter of fact,' he said slowly. 'I asked him that day if he'd swap nights with me and he told me that was why he couldn't.'

'Why did you want to swap nights, sir?'

'We'd been asked out to dinner at short notice by some friends.' He gave him their name.

Had he told anyone else about Dr Somersby playing skittles? — Well, his wife, of course, and their would-be hosts, but no one else that he could remember . . .

Garrett checked over the details again, then let him go.

Connie, when she arrived, expressed similar shock at the possibility of murder.

'It was bad enough him being killed, but this . . . ' She looked up. 'How's Barbara — Mrs Somersby — taking it?'

Pretty much as one would expect, Garrett told her, then asked her about the dispute over Alkovin. Unlike Ian, Connie bridled almost immediately.

'You don't seriously think that that has any bearing on his death, do you, Superintendent?'

'That's what I'm trying to ascertain, doctor.'

She made an irritable gesture, then told him how Leo had approached them first because of Somersby's old-fashioned attitude. Yes, she was sorry they weren't doing the trial, but life goes on ...

'What were you doing last evening, Dr Flint?'

'So I *am* under suspicion?'

Garrett explained again that the questions were for elimination purposes and Connie told him that she'd been at home, nursing her son who had flu.

'He'd come to stay with me for a few days. He began feeling unwell on Monday — which I'd taken off to spend with him — and was really quite ill on Monday night.'

'So you didn't go out on Monday evening?'

Connie looked distinctly embarrassed. 'As a matter of fact, I did, Superintendent. I discovered we'd used the last of the paracetamol in the house — I don't use it much myself. Sebi was running a high temperature, so I drove to a garage shop to buy some.'

'What time would this have been?'

'Around ten, I think. I'm not sure exactly.'

'Couldn't you have asked a neighbour?'

'I could have, but I didn't want to.'

'How long were you out?'

'Twenty minutes, maybe longer.' She gave him the name of the garage and a description of her car.

No, she hadn't known that Dr Somersby was playing skittles that night, and yes, her son was at home now.

'I'd like to see him,' Garrett said.

Connie hesitated. 'He's a lot better than he was, but he's still not well enough to come here.'

'That's all right,' Garrett said equably. 'We'll go and see him.'

She compressed her lips. 'Very well, but please remember he's not well.'

Sebi Flint was up, but didn't look or sound well.

'I'll show a bit more sympathy with people who've had flu in future,' he said with sincerity. 'I've never felt so ill in my life as last night.' He was in his late teens, fair-haired, and would probably have been fresh-faced normally.

Garrett smiled. 'Ah, but I suspect a lot of those who say they've had flu have really only had heavy colds.'

Sebi told him how he'd come down from Manchester University to spend a few days with his father before he went on holiday, and then come to stay with his mother.

'D'you remember your mother going out last night?'

He made a face. 'Dimly. I was pretty much

out of it. I remember her giving me some pills, though.'

*   *   *

The next day, Garrett had Forensic go over their cars: Ian's and his wife's, Connie's and Sebi's, while he tried to locate Leo Farleigh.

Mr Farleigh was away in London, his secretary told him, and had been for several days, but was due back later that day.

Steve Lovell and the sister from Malvern Ward were questioned and confirmed the times that Ian had given, except that Steve hadn't seen Ian when he said he'd come back to the lab. All the department's staff, including Fraser and Terry Stroud, were interviewed, but none of them had anything useful to contribute. The man on duty at the all-night garage remembered Connie coming in to buy the paracetamol at about ten thirty.

Garrett took an almost immediate dislike to Leo when he arrived at the station. Although he was well dressed, he was the type, Garrett thought, who'd have been a spiv in the forties, a ted in the fifties, a mod in the sixties and probably a pusher in the seventies and eighties. So what did that make him now? he wondered.

Yes, he knew about Dr Somersby's death

and was sorry, although he was surprised to hear it might be deliberate ... Yes, he'd spoken to Ian and Connie before Somersby about Alkovin because he'd known what Somersby was like, but he'd been surprised by the firmness with which he'd turned the offer of a trial down.

'It's a wonder drug, Superintendent, it saves lives. Children's lives,' he added virtuously.

'Found anywhere else to try it yet?' Garrett asked, unmoved.

'Yes, a Trust in Birmingham, and I'm working on another in the Smoke.'

''Course, you'll be able to have another go down here now, won't you?'

'I think that would be in rather poor taste, don't you, Superintendent?'

You'll do it all the same, though ... 'Where were you on Monday night?'

'In London. In my hotel from about seven onwards.'

Any witnesses? — Yes, he'd eaten in the hotel restaurant and they'd have a record of that, and he was sure the waiter would remember him.

Then what? — Then he'd gone up to his room, watched telly until about eleven, then gone to bed.

'I thought you reps liked to live it up a bit?'

'We do, usually. But I'd had a hell of a day and was due for another the next.'

* * *

This also checked out. Leo was remembered at dinner, although no one had seen him between eight thirty that evening and eight the next morning.

'If he left London at eight thirty,' Lyn Harvey said, 'he could have made it here by eleven.'

Garrett made a face. 'He'd have had to have pushed it.'

'He could have done it, though. Killed Somersby and then driven back.'

They had Forensic check Leo's car. It was clear, as were all the other cars they'd examined.

'But how do we know which car he was using?' Lyn asked. 'It could have been any of Parc-Reed's fleet. It might have even been a hire car.'

They checked all of Parc-Reed's cars that Leo had access to. Nothing.

They questioned the local car hire firms, but no one of Leo's description, or for that matter, Connie's or Ian's, had hired one that week. They tried to do the same in the area of London where Leo had been staying, but as

Lyn pointed out, Leo could have gone anywhere in London to hire a car.

'In theory, any of them could have physically done it,' Garrett said morosely after a few days, 'just about — *but only if they'd used their own car*. A different car — well, apart from anything else, I don't see how they'd have had the time . . . '

'Unless they hired someone else to kill him,' Lyn said.

'In which case, wouldn't they have made sure they had better alibis?' Garrett asked. 'And there's something else — Saunders may have known about Somersby playing skittles that night, but the others couldn't have.'

'Saunders could have told Farleigh,' Lyn observed. 'Or maybe his wife told someone.'

They had Ian in again and this time grilled him, but other than making him admit that no one had seen him return to the lab after seeing the patient, they couldn't dent his story.

The file had remained open, but over the following weeks and months, with no leads, the enquiry had been gradually wound down. Garrett had even found himself wondering whether it really had been an accident after all, and the perp had then killed Somersby just to make sure he couldn't identify him, or her, later.

5

After two weeks' treatment with DAP, Frances' hair began to fall out and they supplied her with a wig. She also suffered nausea, vomiting and a range of other symptoms which were alleviated (to an extent) by other drugs. Fraser saw her twice a day and sometimes spent the night with her, sleeping in the spare bed put in the room for the purpose.

Connie meticulously kept him up to date with her progress, although for the rest of the time they generally managed to avoid each other.

After eighteen days, the first course of drugs finished and Frances was adjudged to be in remission (an absence of any clinical or laboratory evidence of the disease).

'It's a good sign, isn't it?' she said to Fraser. 'To be in remission so soon.'

'It is,' he said, squeezing her hand. 'A very good sign.'

Remission in anything under four weeks is regarded as good prognostically and Fraser wondered fleetingly whether it would have come so quickly without Alkovin. Ironic if the very thing he'd fought against were to save her life . . . And there was no sign whatever in her of depression or any other neurological symptom.

In fact, she wasn't looking bad at all, he thought. Her grey eyes were clear and if he'd met her in the street, he'd never have known she was wearing a wig — although no wig could match the lustre of her natural hair. Her skin was dry and there were fine lines around her eyes and mouth that made her look a wee bit older, but all in all . . .

'What are you thinking?' she asked.

'Oh, just how good you look.'

'Liar,' she said. Then, 'Thank you,' in almost a whisper. She looked away, said, 'I hope I can feel a bit better now I've stopped the drugs . . . '

They kept her in for a few more days while her neutrophil level (the white cells that are the first defence against infection) built up, then let her go home. Fraser collected her.

'God, it's good to be back,' she said, walking round the living-room, touching the clock on the mantelpiece, the sideboard, the pictures on the walls.

They had an Indian takeaway, and later, when he asked her if she was ready for bed, she said, 'Fancy it, then?'

He looked at her in surprise. 'Sure I do, but are you sure *you* . . . ?'

'I'm not sure of anything,' she said, putting her arms around him. 'I only know I want to feel alive.'

It was very gentle, very slow. She didn't reach orgasm, but she didn't mind that.

A week later, on the evening before she was due back in hospital for 'first consolidation', the second course of DAP, Frances broke down and cried inconsolably, and a clammy hand squeezed at Fraser's heart. He held her, rocked her and after a while she became calmer.

'I'm sorry, I'm sorry, it's just that this week has been so good and the thought of going back on those drugs . . . '

Rational, he thought with relief, *perfectly rational* . . . 'And in three weeks you'll be back here again.'

'Yeah,' she said, trying to smile. 'But you'll stay with me sometimes, won't you?'

'Sure.'

About ten days after that, he was sitting in the office he shared with Mark and Sophie, going through patient files on the computer for the afternoon clinic. He leaned back for a moment, rubbing his eyes and massaging his temples — worry and lack of sleep were accumulating, not helped by the fact that he'd stayed with Frances the night before. She'd been restless all night, tossing, turning, talking in her sleep, and he'd had very little.

'Fraser, hi!'

He looked up to see Leo Farleigh framed in the doorway.

'Oh, hello, Leo.' He hadn't seen him since he'd been back, which was no great loss.

He came in. 'I was so sorry to hear about Frances.'

'Thanks.'

'How is she at the moment?'

'Much as you'd expect.' He took a breath and made an effort to be civil. 'She's ten days into first consolidation, so she's feeling a mite rough at the moment.'

Leo nodded. 'But she went into remission all right?'

'Yes, inside three weeks.'

'Well, that's a hopeful sign.'

'Yeah . . .' *Don't start on about Alkovin.*

He looked back at the computer screen, hoping Leo would take the hint and leave him alone.

But he didn't, he came into the room.

'No sign of any of the — er — symptoms you've been worried about, then?'

'No,' Fraser said shortly.

'Well, that's good news then, isn't it?'

'There's no sign of them *yet* — they tend

to appear after first consolidation.' The muscles on top of his head began tightening, as though there was a weight pressing on it.

Leo said, 'Fraser, it isn't going to happen. I beg you to forget about our disagreements and think positive.'

Go, please just go away . . . Fraser sat perfectly still, not even breathing, but Leo moved closer and said, 'Don't wish it on her, man — Alkovin could be the very thing that — *urggh* . . . '

He was gurgling because Fraser was on his feet with his collar in his hand.

'*Don't* tell me how to think about my fiancée . . . ' He twisted his hand and forced Leo backwards. 'Now, get *out* of here before — '

'What the *hell* is going on?' Ian Saunders appeared in the doorway.

Fraser released his grip and Ian said, 'Into my office, both of you, now.'

He followed them in, shut the door. 'Now, what the hell was that about?'

Leo said quickly, 'I just went to say how sorry I was about Frances and ask how she was and the next thing I knew he was choking me.'

'Fraser?'

'He started lecturing me about Alkovin and in the circumstances it was more than I could take. I lost my temper and I apologise.'

'Is that true, Leo?'

'I was trying to be positive, believe it or not, encouraging.'

'Perhaps not the most tactful scenario,' Ian said.

'I suppose not, although I didn't mean to upset anyone . . . '

'Perhaps you should tell Fraser that.'

'I didn't mean to upset you, Fraser. I'm sorry.'

'All right,' Ian said. 'You'd better go now. I'll speak to you later.'

Leo gratefully withdrew and Ian regarded Fraser for a moment. Then: 'We're all very sorry about what's happened and I can understand the strain you're under, but you can't go about manhandling people. In theory, he could sue you.'

Fraser nodded. 'You're right, Ian, and I'm sorry. It won't happen again.'

'It better not — I mean that, Fraser.'

'It won't,' Fraser repeated.

'OK.' Ian paused. 'You look pretty rough. Did you have a bad night?'

Fraser nodded. 'I stayed with her. She was very restless and I didn't sleep much.'

'Then I'm not surprised you look rough. Why don't you take the rest of the day off and try and get some sleep now?'

70

'Well, Connie's away and there's the clinic this afternoon . . . '

'We'll manage. Go home.'

Fraser went home.

Would things have been any different if Ian had got JS's job instead of Connie? he wondered as he sat back on the sofa with a glass of whisky in his hand.

Maybe, maybe not . . .

They'd run the department more or less as a team both before and after her appointment, but there was no doubt that Connie'd had it in for him ever since the Christmas party . . .

6

December 1997

The disco lights flashed in time with the beat, subtly changing the colour of the shandy in Fraser's glass: red, blue, yellow . . .

'Bloody row,' said Mark Ashcroft, next to him.

'Oh, for God's sake, get a life,' said Chloe, his girlfriend. She was a nurse with straight blonde hair, vivid blue eyes and a heart-stoppingly pretty face. It was the department's Christmas party, a more sumptuous affair than usual because Parc-Reed had added a substantial sum to the slush fund — a 'token of appreciation' of the fact that they'd started the trial on Alkovin.

Leo Farleigh was there; he'd been the life-spirit, if you could call it that, of the party, cracking jokes throughout dinner and playing the obsequious host to Ian and Connie. And now, as Fraser watched, Leo got up and put his hands on the shoulders of Frances, the raven-haired girl, bent and said something to her. She smiled and shook her head. He took her arm and pulled her up. She resisted at first but then, still laughing, allowed him to lead her on to the dance floor.

There was a burst of applause as they began dancing. Leo was wearing a dress shirt of startling whiteness and tight black trousers. He wasn't a big man, maybe an inch or two taller than her five feet six, but he moved like an eel, Fraser thought, weaving his body round her like a spell.

She began to respond. Strobe lights accentuated the darkness of her hair, the pale of her face — it was that that Fraser had noticed about her, the blackness of her hair like curtains round her face . . .

Her face was almost plain compared with, say, Chloe's, but it had far more character, Fraser thought, like her body — that was almost tangible as it moved inside her white dress.

Other couples got up and joined them.

'Come on, Mark,' said Chloe.

'Must I?'

'If you don't, I'll ask Fraser. Would you like to dance with me, Fraser?' She batted her eyes at him, only half joking.

'Oh, all right,' said Mark quickly. They hadn't been going out for very long.

The floor became a jungle. Fraser watched for Leo and Frances, but they were lost in the mêlée.

Leo certainly knew how to get things

moving, he thought wryly. He wondered for a moment about the ethics of Parc-Reed paying for the party, but decided it was probably all right — drug companies had provided sustenance for their customers since medicine began, so why not a disco party?

Ian had become acting director after Somersby's murder. Once the initial shock had passed, he and Connie had approached the Trust's medical committee and said they wanted to take on the Alkovin trial. There were one or two murmurings as to whether the reversal of Somersby's policy so soon after his death was in the best taste, but when the committee heard about the money that might be saved in the future, they quickly agreed.

The murder investigation wound down, and before long it was almost as though JS had never been. Leo was much in evidence, round the department as well as at medical meetings, and Fraser, although he agreed with the trial and its aims, had found the rep's anguilliform pervasiveness increasingly hard to take. So was he an eel, he found himself wondering now, or a lamprey . . . ?

''Ello, sailor,' said a voice, and Connie dropped into a seat beside him. 'Lonely, ducks?'

'Hello, Connie,' he said, pulling himself up.

74

'Can I get you anything?'

'I'm fine, thanks.' She held up a glass of wine and took a mouthful. She was wearing an off-the-shoulder champagne dress that made the most of her breasts and neckline. 'Enjoying yourself?'

'Yes. I've been watching Leo strut his stuff.'

'Yes, he's rather good, isn't he?'

'Multi-talented,' said Fraser, smiling at her.

'You don't like him much, do you, Fraser?'

He briefly pondered a denial, then said, 'How did you know?'

'I've watched you watching him.'

She was watching him now and he thought, *She's had a few* . . . Maybe it was *she* who was lonely.

She looked over at the writhing mass of dancers. 'It's like an organism, isn't it?' she said. 'With a life of its own.'

'Waiting to swallow us all, perhaps.'

'With Leo at its nucleus?'

'I hadn't thought of him in that way.'

'It hasn't swallowed you yet, has it, Fraser?'

'Oh, I'm not much of a dancer.'

'No, it's not the foremost of your attributes, is it?'

She smiled as she said it and he realised several things at once: she'd made reference to Birmingham, she'd done so quite deliberately and she was his for the asking.

And it wasn't just his brain that knew, it was his body as well. He could feel himself hardening in sympathy — it had been a long time and for a moment he was tempted . . .

No. It was a bad idea, and when it came down to it, he didn't really want her . . .

He was rescued from having to say anything by the return of Mark and Chloe.

'Hello, Connie,' Mark said. 'Can I get you a drink?'

'No, thank you, Mark, I was just going.' She emptied her wine glass and put it on the table. 'To be swallowed,' she added with a smile.

'What did she mean, swallowed?' Chloe asked Fraser.

He explained, watching as Connie tapped Leo on the shoulder and said something to him. Frances, the raven-haired girl, withdrew — not ungratefully, it seemed to Fraser. Connie and Leo began dancing and disappeared into the crowd.

Well, that's all right then, Fraser thought, relieved.

Frances looked over at him suddenly as she reached her table and smiled at him, and without thinking, he got up and went over to her.

'Would you like me to take over?'

'To be honest, I'm flaked.'

'I'm nothing like such hard work as Leo.'

'Oh, all right.'

In the midst of the organism, where his lack of grace didn't show, Fraser was rather enjoying himself until he suddenly bumped into someone.

'Sorry,' he mouthed, then realised it was Connie.

She didn't reply, just shot him a look of pure malevolence before disappearing in the press of bodies.

Oh dear, he thought. *Not all right* . . .

Frances had seen it too and was looking at him quizzically . . . then the music came to an end and Ian, who'd been lurking in the background, took the microphone from the DJ and made a short speech, thanking Parc-Reed for their hospitality.

The party went on, but Fraser decided to leave before he could do his career any more damage.

★   ★   ★

Early in January, to everyone's astonishment — including, apparently, her own — Connie got the job as director. The rumour was put about, some said by Connie herself, that the Trust, tired of hearing that they'd never appoint a woman, decided to prove 'them' wrong. Ian seemed to take it equably and they continued to run the department in tandem.

One of her first acts as director was to send Fraser away to a hospital in Bath for three months. It was something he'd known was going to happen, and he had no objection, but he couldn't rid himself of the feeling that he was being sent away as a punishment.

★ ★ ★

In Fraser's dream, no sooner had he picked up one phone than another took over from it, so that when he did become awake enough to snatch up the real thing, he couldn't quite believe it when the ringing stopped.

'Dr Callan,' he said, unsure that he'd be answered.

'Fraser, it's Frances Templeton. I'm at the lab. Brian Goodman's been brought into A and E with slashed wrists.'

'Ach, *shit!* — Sorry, Frances . . . ' He was on call, having been back from Bath for three weeks.

'He's in Resus. now, but his platelet count's only nineteen. He's A pos and we've got one adult platelet dose, but only two units of blood that are irradiated, leukodepleted and CMV neg. I've issued them, but they've asked for red label — '

'*Don't* let them have ordinary blood, whatever you do. Order some more irradiated from the transfusion centre.'

'I've done that and it should be here in a quarter of an hour. Shall I cross match it or issue it red label?'

'Start the cross match while I go and see him. I'll be with you as soon as I can.'

He glanced at the clock as he quickly dressed — nearly one — then, still swearing, he drove to the hospital.

He should have seen it coming. Brian Goodman was in his fifties and had been diagnosed with acute lymphoblastic leukaemia three months earlier. He'd been put on DAP and within three weeks was in remission. He'd been a cheerful, optimistic man, not particularly intelligent, but determined to 'have a crack' at beating the disease.

Then, after his first consolidation, he'd become withdrawn and morose. His wife said he was depressed, but Goodman himself insisted there was nothing wrong and refused the offer of antidepressants.

They should have found some way of persuading him, Fraser thought now — Goodman was naturally the kind of man who'd think admitting to depression wimpish.

79

He arrived at Accident and Emergency and the harassed young house officer in Resuscitation told him how Goodman had been found in the bath by his wife.

'It's only one wrist, but very deep. He's lost a lot of blood.'

'What have you given him?'

'Haemocell and two units of blood. He's having the platelets now, but he desperately needs more blood.'

'You can have some more in — ' he looked at his watch — 'half an hour.' Seeing the look on her face, he said, 'In his state, it's not worth the risk of infection or transfusion reaction to give him red label. Is he conscious?'

She shook her head. 'He's in there if you want to see him.' She indicated a curtained cubicle. 'His wife's with him.'

She was on one side of the bed, holding his hand, and a staff nurse was on the other. The shallow rise and fall of his chest was the only sign that he was still human. His wife said, 'Can I speak to you, doctor?'

He took her to a corner and she told him how he'd seemed much happier that day. 'I should have guessed it was because he'd made his mind up to do this . . . ' He'd told her he was going to have a bath and that she should go to bed. She'd dozed off, then woken to find herself alone and gone to look for him.

'Oh, the silly old fool . . . ' She wept briefly, then said, 'Will he be all right, doctor?'

'I think so, once we've got some more blood into him.'

He went back to the bedside with her, then walked over to the lab and found Frances.

'Has the blood arrived yet?'

She nodded. 'Should be ready in about twenty minutes.'

'Well done.'

'Have you seen him?'

'Yes, and his wife.'

'What made him do it? He was doing so well . . . '

'I know.' He repeated what Mrs Goodman had told him.

She said, 'I didn't think they did slash their wrists if they really meant it, I thought it was usually a cry for help.'

'Oh, he meant it fine well, he used a Stanley knife.'

'Ugh.' She shuddered. 'Poor man. His poor wife.'

'In a way, it fits in with his personality.'

'How d'you mean?'

'Old-fashioned, too proud to admit he was depressed, using what he saw as a macho way to finish himself off.'

'Will it affect his chances?'

'Well, it won't help them.'

A timer went off and she went to see to the cross match.

On impulse, he followed her. 'Can I help?'

She looked at him in mild surprise. 'D'you know how to issue blood through the computer?'

He shook his head.

'Then thanks, but not really.'

'Can I make you a coffee, then?'

'Not coffee — I'll never sleep. A glass of squash would be nice.'

The phone rang. She picked it up, said 'Yes' a few times and wrote some details down, then replaced it and turned back to Fraser. 'There's another cross match on its way, so perhaps I will have that coffee.'

She joined him in the rest room fifteen minutes later.

'All done?' he asked.

She nodded as she sat down. 'Six units.'

'That should see him through.' He got up and made the coffee. She'd taken off her lab coat and was wearing jeans and a T-shirt. She wasn't wearing a bra, he noticed — she'd probably just got into bed when she was called. 'Milk and sugar?' he asked.

'Just milk, please.'

He handed it to her.

'Thanks.' She took a sip. After a short silence, she said, 'Pleased to be back with us?'

'Yes, I am.'

'How did you like Bath?'

'It's a fine city.'

'But not really for you.'

'How did you know?'

She shrugged. 'Your expression.'

He smiled, said, 'It's fine, beautiful place, a bit like Edinburgh. But it's somehow a mite pleased with itself, complacent.'

'Also a bit like Edinburgh?'

'Aye.' He grinned at her — she was leaning back in her seat, her head slightly to one side, holding her coffee cup in both hands between her thighs. 'You've been there?' he asked.

She nodded, then said, 'How long have you got with us now?'

'Three years and a bit.'

'So where d'you think you'll go after that?'

'Anywhere that'll have me, within reason.'

'Not back to Scotland?'

He took a mouthful of coffee before answering. 'I don't think so. There are more opportunities in England.'

'You don't miss Scotland?'

Again, he paused. 'That's a bit like asking an East Ender whether he misses England. What about you?' he continued quickly. 'Have you not been tempted to move on? To better things?'

She smiled briefly, recognising the equivocal nature of the question, but took her time to reply.

'Events have conspired to keep me here,' she said at last. 'At the moment — it's my mother — my father died last year and — '

'I'm sorry to hear that.'

'Thanks. It would hurt her if I moved away just now, especially as my brother's living abroad.' She spoke with a slight, but perceptible Avonian accent, rather attractive.

'You could always move to one of the other labs round here.'

'Easily, if I was prepared to downgrade, which I'm not. Besides, that kind of move usually involves swapping one set of problems for another. And anyway — ' she smiled to show him she knew what he was getting at — 'Terry doesn't bother me so much as he does some of the others.'

'I've noticed,' he said. Then: 'What kept you here before your mother?'

He immediately regretted asking the question, but was saved by the buzzer at the lab entrance.

'That'll be the sample for the cross match,' she said, getting up.

He watched as she left the room — her

T-shirt had rucked up slightly over her backside and the sight of it as she walked away sent a shot of pure gold into his veins.

He washed up the mugs, then went to find her.

'I'll take another look at Brian, then I'll be away,' he said. 'I hope you're not up all night.'

'So do I.' She smiled. 'Thanks for the coffee.'

'My pleasure.'

Goodman still hadn't regained consciousness, although his colour had improved and his breathing was easier. Fraser reasured his wife again, then drove home.

Sleep wouldn't come. Images flickered: her face with its delicate colours framed by her dark, almost black hair, the T-shirt painted over her body, her long legs . . .

He got up, padded naked downstairs and poured himself a whisky. *Lust?* he wondered as he sipped. *Something more?*

He'd had a brief and rather unsatisfactory affair in Bath with a nursing sister called Emma. She'd been clever, sophisticated and superficial. A girl. Whereas Frances, for all he'd thought of her as the raven-haired girl, was a woman . . . How old would she be? She was a Senior, so she'd have to be twenty-five . . . and he'd have bet anything that the other 'event conspiring' was a long-term affair . . .

Was she interested?

More to the point, was he? Did he really want an affair with someone he worked with?

Aye, he rather thought he might in this case ... although Connie wouldn't approve of him fraternising with the lab staff.

And there was something else Connie wasn't going to like, he remembered — having resolved one problem in his mind, he turned it to another.

The next day, between clinics, he spent an hour going over patient records in the computer, then another on the phone. Then he went to Connie's room.

'Can I have a word?'

'Of course you can, Fraser. Come and sit down.'

He closed the door and sat. 'You'll have heard about Brian Goodman?'

'Yes, Ian told me. D'you think he meant it?'

'Yes, I do.' He explained why. 'The thing is, Connie, I've been looking back over the records and I'm beginning to wonder whether maybe JS was right.'

'Right about what?'

'Alkovin causing severe psychotic effects.'

She frowned. 'You'd better explain.'

In the four treatment centres in the area, he told her, they'd had twenty-one cases of ALL treated with DAP in the last nine months, and in ten of these the patients had suffered from depression. In three of them, they'd also suffered from paranoia and/or dementia.

'Is that all, Fraser? I'd have expected *all* of them to be depressed, not just ten.'

'I'm talking about clinical depression, occuring — '

'How exactly d'you define that?'

'Profound, prolonged, accompanied by feelings of guilt and self-blame — not to mention suicide.'

'The fact is, Fraser, people do tend to have these feelings when they're told they've got leukaemia.'

This was turning out to be even more difficult than he'd thought. 'The symptoms I'm talking about are occuring after consolidation, not immediately — '

'That's a list of them, is it?' She nodded at the paper in his hands. 'Can I see?'

He handed it over and she quickly scanned it.

'How many of these have you actually seen for yourself?'

'About half,' he admitted.

'So your diagnosis of severe psychosis applies to only five patients, not ten.'

'I've checked on the others inasmuch as I can — '

'There's been nothing in the literature — has there?'

'Not so far as I know.'

'Haven't you checked?'

'Not yet.' He silently cursed himself.

'Well, don't you think you should?'

'I take your point, Connie, and I will. But I still think we should look into it.'

'You check the literature and I'll have a word with Ian about it. But I do suggest you check your facts more thoroughly in future before raising alarms like this.'

A week later, Connie convened a meeting in her room with Fraser, Ian, Leo and Robert Swann, the new consultant. She started by asking Fraser to reiterate his concerns about Alkovin, which he did. He hadn't found anything in the medical journals, although he had researched further into some of the cases.

The husband of one patient had told him how his wife had threatened suicide and that he was convinced she'd meant it. Antidepressants had helped her. And a woman had told him how her husband had suddenly become violent, hitting her and then threatening her with a kitchen knife. Afterwards, he'd broken down and begged forgiveness and a day or so later had apparently erased the whole thing from his mind. Both patients had subsequently relapsed and died.

After a moment of silence, Connie said, 'Tragic though these cases are, we must remember that we're dealing with people who have, effectively, been told they're likely to die. We can all produce anecdotes of patients who, in similar circumstances, have behaved outrageously — because, with respect, Fraser, that's all you've given us — anecdotes.'

She and Ian had been busy as well and had the advantage that, between them, they had seen all the patients involved. They went systematically through all the others on Fraser's list. Yes, they'd suffered from depression, but in their view, not to any exceptional degree. Even episodes of violence were not uncommon in very sick people. The only possible exception was Brian Goodman . . .

'Attempted suicide is far from unknown in leukaemia,' Ian said, 'and it was only a matter of time before our turn came round.' He turned to Leo. 'They've had a lot more experience using the drug in America. We haven't found anything in the literature — have you heard of anything from the trials there?'

'Not a thing,' Leo replied — predictably, Fraser thought.

Sure, patients with leukaemia got

depressed, maybe even a little psychotic occasionally — Prednisolone had been known to have mild effects of this nature.

Robert, who hadn't said much until now, spoke up.

'Since Fraser's seen fit to raise this problem — '

'*Alleged* problem,' Leo corrected.

'All right, alleged problem,' Robert agreed. 'The thing is, it can't hurt for us to keep an eye on things, be ready to treat with antidepressants as soon as any symptoms appear, maybe even prophylactically in some — '

'I'm not keen on prophylactic treatment,' Connie interrupted. 'By all means treat symptoms when, and if, they arise, but to treat them before they even appear would be to wish the problem on us.'

Which is all damn fine, Fraser thought a few minutes later when the meeting ended, *but* . . . But, when it came down to it, he'd achieved nothing except to lower himself a few more yards in Connie's estimation.

Serves you right for sleeping with the boss, he told himself, although, as he remembered it, there hadn't been a deal of sleeping.

He started towards his office without much idea of what he was going to do there when he saw Frances making for the way out. On impulse, he followed and caught up with her in the corridor.

'Going to lunch?'

'Into town. Shopping.' She sounded in a hurry.

'Ah . . . ' A poster he'd seen on the way to work floated into his mind and he said, 'There's a Stoppard on at the Foundry I'd like to see. Would you like to come with me?'

She'd stopped, looked at him without expression for a moment, then she'd said, 'Yes, I would.'

7

July 1999

She was home from hospital again, for ten days, and Fraser had taken time off. The treatment had put new lines round her mouth now, giving her face a slightly pouched look, adding several years to it.

'I'm sorry, but I don't think I could,' she said in bed, a small voice, when he ran his fingers over her breast. 'Please, just hold me.'

She didn't want to go out, she just read or watched TV. On the second evening, he made a lasagne, one of her favourites. She took a couple of mouthfuls and put her fork down.

'It's very nice, Fraser, but I'm not really hungry.'

'Are you all right?'

Her face soured as she stared at him and her mouth pursed. 'God, you have no *idea* how sick I am of hearing that phrase — *Are you all right?*' she mimicked. '*Are you all right?* . . . Of course I'm not fucking all right, I've got fucking leukaemia, haven't I?'

She made to get up and go, but he caught her wrist.

'We've got to talk about this, Frances — '

She snatched her hand away. 'Leave me *alone* . . . and get something into your head, I am not fucking depressed — OK?' Without warning, she picked up her plate and propelled it into his face as though it were a custard pie, then she stared open-mouthed at him for a moment before collapsing on to her arms on the table, weeping hysterically.

'*Help me please Fraser help me help me help me* . . .'

He hurried round the table, trying to wipe the mess from his face with a serviette. He pulled up a chair, sat beside her. 'I'll help you, please let me . . .'

She threw her arms round his neck. 'Please, please help me . . .'

After a while, when he'd calmed her down, he left her on the sofa and phoned his GP's surgery. His doctor was there, but with a patient. Fraser asked the receptionist if he could call back, urgently. He came back to him after five minutes, listened, then said he'd be there as soon as he finished his appointments.

He was there in an hour. He examined Frances, listened to Fraser, then prescribed Prozac and a sedative to help her sleep.

Fraser put her to bed and stayed with her, waiting for it to work. When she was asleep, he went downstairs. He knew there would be no sleep for him that night without bottled assistance.

She was still sleeping when he woke in the morning, turned towards him and snoring slightly. Sleep had smoothed the lines round her mouth so that, with her hairless head, she looked like a baby, so vulnerable that he lay there watching her for a while.

Fraser didn't feel too bad, considering the booze he'd put away the night before, although there was an ominous fuzziness around his forehead. He showered, hoping the jets of water would drive it away, which they did for a while. She woke as he dressed.

'What time is it?' she asked drowsily.

'Half-past eight.' He sat on the bed beside her. 'How are you feeling?'

'OK.' She looked up at him. 'Why do you ask me like that?'

He studied her face. 'You don't remember last night?'

Her brow furrowed. 'Oh . . . did we have a row? I thought it was a dream.'

'You don't remember Dr Parker coming here?'

'No . . . we had a row and then you put me to bed . . . didn't you?'

'D'you not remember what happened in between?'

She shook her head.

'Well, it was some row.' He thought quickly, decided it was best to tell her the truth . . .

'Wow,' she said when he finished. 'And you think it's the Alkovin?'

He nodded. 'I'm sure of it.'

'Me — on Prozac. Wow — so I've finally made it. To the middle classes,' she explained at his puzzled expression.

'Yeah.' He grinned. 'So how *are* you feeling?'

'Not much different from yesterday. Pissed off. Glad you're here. How long does it take to work?'

'Prozac? Anything between one and three weeks.'

'Well, let's hope — '

The phone rang and he picked it up.

'It's your mother,' he said, handing it to her. 'D'you want some tea?'

She nodded as she took it from him.

He was at the door when she said, 'She wants to come round — that's OK, isn't it?'

An hour later, when mother and daughter were ensconced in the sitting-room over coffee, Fraser mumbled something non-committal and slipped out. He went straight to the hospital and Connie's room.

'I thought you were on leave, Fraser.'

'I am. I came in to tell you that Frances

had a breakdown last night.'

'How d'you mean, a breakdown?'

'Our GP diagnosed severe depression. He's put her on Prozac and a sedative.'

'I'm very sorry to hear that, Fraser,' she said carefully. 'However, I do think I should have been consulted about it.'

'Why? So that you could have refused her treatment?'

'Don't be ridiculous. So that, as her consultant, I could have assessed her condition and treated her accordingly.'

'The treatment of severe depression is well enough — '

'I might have decided on a different drug, one with sedative properties, perhaps. I might well have thought counselling more appropriate — '

'Counselling!' The fuzziness returned, twisting the muscles round his forehead. 'For Christ's sake, she's depressed to the extent of being disturbed — '

'Perhaps you could describe her symptoms, preferably without shouting.'

He swallowed, forced himself to relax, and told her, not holding anything back. Connie regarded him coolly from behind her desk, her face smooth, impassive, unemotional. She said, 'I won't alter the medication, now it's been prescribed and she's taking it, but I do very strongly recommend counselling. For both of you,' she added.

'I beg your pardon?'

'You heard me.'

'You're suggestin' that *I* need — '

'This is a very stressful time for both of you. It's bound to affect your relationship, which has to be a major factor in the symptoms you describe.' She stood up. 'And now — '

'I don't think you're in any position to be a judge of anyone's relationship, Connie, let alone mine.'

'You'd better explain that, Fraser.' Her voice was still, her face expressionless.

'I don't have to explain *anything* to you, Connie, not a damned thing. You are the one — ' he pointed — 'who's going to have to explain why you persisted with the use of a drug with dangerous side-effects.'

She laughed. 'Put your finger away, Fraser, you look silly like that. And you'll sound silly, *very* silly if you try to bring that old chestnut up again.' She came round from her desk, moving towards the door. 'You don't seem to have grasped yet that Alkovin may, *if* we're lucky, enable me to save your girlfriend's life.' She stopped, about a yard away from him. 'I don't expect gratitude, but I would have hoped for more professional respect, even from one of your background.'

He absorbed this, then said, 'You asked me to explain myself just now. What I meant was that bein' a failure at relationships yourself, you are now tryin' to undermine one that's success — '

She caught him a ringing slap on the side of his face that knocked him sideways, then another on the other cheek without giving him the option of turning it first . . . and there would have been more, but for the fact he seized her wrists and held them.

'Let go of me,' she hissed into his face.

He gripped harder. 'Not until you — '

She brought her knee up into his groin. He gasped, dropped her wrists as she let out a piercing scream and ran to the door.

'Help! Ian, he's assaulting me . . . '

Fraser painfully straightened himself up as Ian came running in.

'Connie . . . what in God's name . . . Fraser . . . ?'

'He assaulted me, Ian,' Connie said breathlessly. 'Get the police.'

'Surely we don't need — '

'He came in here shouting about Frances, then he grabbed me — look . . . ' She held up her wrists, which were already beginning to bruise where he'd gripped her.

'If there was any assault, it was she who

assaulted me,' Fraser said, aware as he said it of how feeble it sounded.

'I was trying to defend myself,' Connie said. 'Call the police, Ian, now. If you don't, I will.'

By now, several other faces were peering in through the door — Robert, Sophie, Terry Stroud.

'Oh, Jesus wept,' said Ian despairingly. He phoned the police.

They came and took statements. Fraser was told he could go home and was advised to stay there. He knew he had to tell the British Medical Association, the doctors' trade union, what had happened, and thought about doing it from a phone box, so as to avoid worrying Frances or Mary, then realised they would have to know sooner or later anyway.

Both women listened slack-mouthed to his account. Frances knew about their relationship, so it wasn't quite so much of a shock for her, but Fraser didn't care for the way Mary's look became increasingly askance.

'I have to say that Dr Flint struck me as the last kind of person who would do such a thing,' she said.

'Well, it doesn't surprise me,' Frances said. 'She's a complete bitch underneath all the charm.' She sighed. 'I wish you'd told me

99

where you were going, Fraser.'

'So that you could have stopped me, I suppose?'

'Too damn right.'

He pressed his lips together, then said, 'Well, so do I, now.'

'It'll sort itself out,' she said.

But after Mary had gone, she said, 'It's a mess, isn't it?'

'I'll not be allowed to go on working there.'

'No, you won't. Would they let you go to one of the other hospitals in the region to finish your contract?'

'I don't know.'

'D'you think Ian believed her?'

'I don't know that either. Why?'

'Would he give you a reference?'

'He might,' Fraser said slowly. 'It's in their interest to get rid of me as quietly as possible.'

They talked over their options during the rest of the afternoon. Fraser couldn't help noticing that his problems had, paradoxically, seemed to lift Frances' mood, so much so that they went out for a meal that evening. Later, though, she became spiky and unstable again and it took all his diplomacy to avoid another row. At least she agreed to take the sedative, which helped her to sleep — that night, and over the weekend.

On Monday, after a visit to the Trust HQ where an administrator told him he was suspended on full pay, he went to the small office the BMA had in the city.

'You realise, Dr Callan, that as an organisation we represent both you and Dr Flint?' Dr Smith was earnest, bespectacled and, underneath his elderly medical student image, rather shrewd. 'So it's in our interest to find a compromise, one that suits both of you. What is *not* in our interest is the public spectacle of two professionals fighting. You do see that, don't you?'

'Sure I do,' Fraser said. 'But I will not, *cannot*, compromise my position on Alkovin. It's a dangerous drug.'

Smith considered him, then said, 'Tell me about it again — how, exactly, did it come to be used in your department?'

He listened carefully while Fraser went through it in detail, putting in questions now and again.

At last he said, 'I'm going to give you the phone number of some people in London who may be able to help you provided you forget it was me who gave it you.'

Fraser rang it as soon as he got home and was put through to someone with the unlikely name of Tom Jones.

'Can you come up on Wednesday?' Jones

asked after Fraser briefly told him what it was about. He had a marked London accent.

Fraser asked Frances who shrugged and said, 'All right.' She looked so miserable after he put the phone down that he went and put his arms around her.

After a few moments, he said quietly, 'Why don't we get married?'

'We are, in September.'

'No, I mean this week. Get a special licence and just have your mother and maybe one or two others.'

Her expression went from astonishment to delight. 'What a lovely idea . . . ' She thought about it, savouring it for a while, then sighed. 'We've told everyone September, and I think it would be unlucky to change it. But thank you.'

She was probably right, he thought, it might give the wrong message to rush things.

It was strange how he'd known what he'd wanted from the time he first took her out . . .

8

May 1998 – January 1999
I could marry this one . . .

The thought had come from nowhere and he'd laughed softly at himself as he'd brought the drinks over.

'Share the joke?' she'd said as he sat down.

'Oh, just something in the play,' he lied, and picked an incident at random from the Stoppard they'd just seen.

He'd had plenty of girlfriends, but never such a thought before. It wasn't as if she was startlingly pretty, he'd had prettier, but there was something about her face, the way it lit when she smiled, that entranced him . . .

'What made you decide to go for medicine?' she asked. 'I've never met a lab worker who became a doctor before, let alone a pathologist.'

He thought for a moment. 'I suppose it was when I was doing my part-time degree — did you do that?'

She shook her head. 'I did mine full-time at university. You were saying . . . ?'

'Well, I could see the others struggling with stuff I was soaking up — sorry if this sounds big-headed, I thought at the time there must be some catch . . . but then, when I passed with first class honours having not exactly killed myself studying, I realised I had a facility for exams and decided to push it as far as it would go.'

'How sickening,' she said. 'I'd have been one of the strugglers. But what made you choose medicine?'

He shrugged. 'I found the human body, its workings, fascinating — it's why I went into lab work in the first place.'

'But how did you manage to get into medical school? I thought they only took people who got straight As at school.'

'They do make exceptions, but it was mostly due to the pathologist where I worked, Dr McCloud.' He told her how he'd encouraged him, taken the time to show him how to approach the interviews, the kind of answers they liked. 'I'd never have done it without him.' He smiled. 'He had no preconceptions, he took people entirely on their own merits.'

'You make him sound a bit like JS.'

Fraser smiled again, mirthlessly this time. 'Aye, maybe he was.'

'And now it's all change,' she said tonelessly.

'Yeah.'

She said, 'Have you noticed? Nobody ever seems to talk about him now — it's almost as though there's a tacit conspiracy . . . '

'I can think of one reason for that.'

She looked at him.

'Because if it *wasn't* an accident . . . Can you remember who the police spent the most time with?'

'No?'

'Connie, Ian and Leo. They must have had their reasons for that.'

'No,' she said, shaking her head. 'No, I can't believe that. Let's talk about something else.'

Later, when he stopped outside her house, she said, 'Thanks for a lovely evening, Fraser.'

'I'd like to see you again.'

'You will, tomorrow.'

'That's not what I meant.'

'I know.' She quickly kissed him on the side of the mouth before climbing out of the car.

He watched her go in. She waved as she shut the door.

★ ★ ★

They disagreed about foxhunting, emotional intelligence, hand guns and South American politics.

'You could always stay the night,' he suggested.

'Thank you — ' she smiled that smile — 'but I think I'll go home.'

They agreed about Tony Blair, Mozart, the sea and South African politics.

'Stay with me . . . '

'Don't push me, Fraser.'

Yes, she'd lived with someone before, for nearly a year, investing more than she'd got in return, which was why, when she did stay with him, it was at a time of her own choosing.

* * *

'I don't believe you,' she said. 'Show me.'

The one-piece swimming costume clung to her body like sealskin and he suddenly felt a childish desire to show off.

He took several deep breaths, then ducked under the water and began swimming away from her; soon she couldn't see him for the ripples made by the other swimmers. About half a minute later he bobbed up at the far end of the swimming pool over a hundred feet away. She swam over and joined him. He was still panting.

'Where did you learn to do that?' she asked.

'Used to go swimming a lot.' He grinned at her between breaths. 'In Glasgae, if y' didnae like footba', there was only swimming left.'

'Most people prefer to swim *on* the water, not *under* it.'

He shrugged. 'It's just something I've always liked doing. I did a diving course in Israel a few years ago.'

'Why Israel?'

'Why not? It's hot and the life under the Red Sea is . . . well, y' have to see it to believe it.'

'D'you still go there?'

'I went last year. Why? Fancy coming with me?'

'I might.'

Later, in the pub, he asked her about her family. Her father had been a teacher, she told him, her mother too, until they married.

'Dad could have been a headmaster if he'd been prepared to move, but Mum wouldn't leave Avon.'

'Roots?'

'Deep ones in her case — I've lost count of the number of cousins twice removed I've got round here.'

'It didn't stop your brother moving away — Africa, isn't it?'

'Botswana. He's a teacher too and he loves it there. He comes home every Christmas, burnt to a cinder, but you can see he's itching to get back.'

'Older than you?'

She nodded, then looked at him curiously. 'D'you ever see your family? You never mention them . . . '

He shrugged and looked away. 'I try to see my mother at Christmas, but . . . '

'Yes?' she prompted.

'I know it sounds bad, but she always has my brothers over when I'm there an' I'm . . . I'm not comfortable with them. Nor they with me. I don't really belong there.'

She half smiled. 'You make it sound as though you're a refugee from a foreign country.'

'Have you ever been to Glasgow?'

She shook her head. 'But I thought it was supposed to be the cultural centre of Europe now,' she said innocently.

Fraser snorted. 'Now that would depend on which bit you were in and who you might be listening to. Would you jump at the chance of an invite to a social gathering in St Paul's?'

'Aren't you being rather judgemental?'

He didn't reply and she said, 'I suppose not, but every city's got its dodgy areas, hasn't it?'

'Aye, an' I grew up in one,' he said quietly. 'It's fine well for a person to drive through an' say, 'Oh, what an interesting community', but they wouldn't want to live there.'

The bitterness in his voice surprised her, but she didn't say anything, sensing that he would go on.

'Remember how I told you I was good at academic work? Well, in the school I went to, that was the quickest way to social oblivion. Even my brothers were embarrassed by me.' He paused again, then seemed to come to a decision and went on: 'The only way I could gain any kind of street cred was to prove myself by my deeds out of school. So — ' he took a breath, released it — 'I joined a gang of joyriders, learned how to break into cars, hot wire the engines an' drive round like a maniac terrorising people.'

'How old were you?'

'Fourteen, fifteen.'

'Hormones,' she said. 'Testosterone.'

He shrugged again. 'Maybe.'

'Didn't you get caught?'

'Eventually, which was probably the best thing could have happened.' He smiled without humour. 'My form teacher came to court and spoke for me and I only got probation. But you know what really got me? The old man whose car I'd stolen had to come to court to give evidence, and when I looked at him, I saw what I'd become. When I promised never to do it again, I meant it.'

'Did you keep the promise?'

'Aye. But I had no real friends after that and just lived for the time I could get out.' He looked up at her. 'That's why I don't belong there an' hate going back. And yet, I'm not sure I belong here, either.'

'Yes you do,' she said, but they both knew what he meant.

★ ★ ★

'Did you know that Fraser and Frances Templeton are virtually living together?' Ian watched Connie's face as he imparted this information.

'I believe I'd heard a rumour,' Connie said disinterestedly. 'I'm glad he's found his level,' she added, which told Ian what he wanted to know.

Fraser didn't care what they thought. He didn't care about anything else much and it wasn't until after Frances had moved in with him that he gave Alkovin any more consideration.

It was another suicide attempt, successful this time; a man of fifty who had relapsed after consolidation.

'I'm sure Fraser's eyes would have lit up when he heard about it,' Connie said at the weekly medical meeting, 'but I think we can agree that this man's personal life, taken together with the relapse, is explanation enough.'

'My eyes would never light up for anyone's death,' Fraser felt impelled to say. 'Especially a suicide.'

'Of *course* not, Fraser. I was joking.'

The meeting moved on, but Fraser noticed that Robert Swann, the junior consultant, had been on the point of saying something and then apparently changed his mind. He was a quiet, almost withdrawn man, younger than Fraser, but they seemed to get on.

Over the next month, Fraser wrote up every case of psychosis in ALL he could find and compared the number with that in myeloid leukaemia, which wasn't treated with Alkovin. There was a statistically significant increase with ALL.

Then, although he knew he was taking a risk, he contacted his opposite number in Birmingham and asked if he could see the data in their Alkovin trial.

They hadn't been looking for it in the same way, but there was nevertheless a significantly higher rate of neurological disturbance where Alkovin was used.

He considered approaching one of the higher managers in the Trust, then thought he'd have a better chance of convincing them if he had someone else on his side. He went to see Robert.

'Forgive me if I'm wrong,' he fished, 'but I've gained the impression that you might have reservations about the Alkovin situation.'

After a pause, Robert nibbled carefully. 'Some of the things you've come up with have made me wonder once or twice.' After a pause, he said, 'Put it this way, Fraser — I can't see that it would hurt to take a look at it. Use reverse criteria perhaps, assume there *is* a neurological effect and look for evidence.'

To commit himself or not? Fraser wondered . . .

'Well, the fact is, Robert, I've done just that. Looked for and found evidence.'

'*Have* you now? Is that it there?' He nodded at the sheaf of paper in Fraser's hands.

'I've made you a copy.'

They went through it together and Fraser told him what he had in mind.

'I need to think about it,' Robert said. 'Can I keep this?'

'Sure.'

He didn't keep Fraser waiting long. Late the next morning, he was summoned to Connie's room. Connie and Ian were there, Fraser's results in front of them.

'Robert very sensibly brought this to us,' she said without preamble. 'How *dare* you go behind my back, approach other hospitals without my permission?' She was shaking with anger, he noticed.

He looked straight back at her. 'I dared because I believe, as did John Somersby, that there is something seriously wrong with Alkovin and — '

'And we have repeatedly told you that there *isn't*. Are you calling us liars?'

'No,' he said carefully, 'I am not, but I believe you to be mistaken.'

'It is *you* who are mistaken, Fraser. We've looked into all the cases you brought to our attention and satisfied ourselves that there was nothing out of the ordinary. We even approached the manufacturers, who have looked into the matter and found nothing. What more do you want?'

'If that's a serious question, then an independent enquiry — '

'Isn't our word good enough for you? We've looked at this long and hard and found absolutely nothing.'

'And I've discovered the same problem in Birmingham.'

'Exactly!' Connie said. 'The same *non-*problem. If you were to examine this — ' she slapped the paper in front of her — 'properly, case by case, instead of jumping to conclusions, then you would find the same set of explanations. *There is not a problem.*'

Fraser tried to keep his face impassive as he pondered the impossibility of countering such conviction. He was saved from having to say anything by Ian.

'You know the first aphorism of research, don't you, Fraser? Any research.'

'I'm sure you're about to enlighten me.'

'If you look for something, you'll find it. Think about it, Fraser. Once you'd got this idea into your head, you started looking for more cases — and lo! You found them. It's subjective. What Connie and I see as normal human reactions to a life-threatening disease, you see as evidence of psychosis. Take the time to think about it, ask yourself some honest questions.'

'Isn't there a corollary to your aphorism?' Fraser said before he could stop himself. 'If you blind yourself to something, then you won't see it.'

Connie looked as though she'd explode with fury. 'That's it, I've had enough — ' but Ian put a hand on her arm.

'And that's what you think we're doing, is it, Fraser? Deliberately blinding our eyes to the problem? That wasn't a rhetorical question,' he added after a pause.

114

'I don't know what to think any more,' Fraser said.

'We haven't convinced you?'

'I'm afraid not.'

'So where do we go from here?' He said it almost as though musing to himself, then looked at Connie.

'Clearly we can't go on like this,' she said, 'so we've decided to give you a cooling-off period. I've written a memo to the Trust management explaining that you're going on a three-month sabbatical to the Western Hospital in Seattle, America.'

Fraser gazed at them. 'But what if I don't want to — '

'That is not an option. If you refuse to go, then we will take steps to terminate your contract. I'm quite aware that that would mean unpleasantness for *all* of us, but that's what we'll do.' She allowed a wintry smile to touch her lips. 'As the Americans themselves say, you'd better believe it.'

They had given him until the next morning to think about it. He'd talked it over with Frances and then accepted. A week later, he'd been in America.

9

July 1999

'And the irony is,' Fraser told Marcus Evans now, 'that it was there I found the evidence that finally convinced me.'

'How did that come about?'

Marcus Evans was the Compleat Civil Servant, Fraser thought: dark suit, sober tie, shirt from an advert for washing powder and a bald head with heavy moustache to compensate; the only off-key note was the sense of humour lurking around his eyes and mouth.

Once in Seattle, Fraser told him, he'd remembered John Somersby talking about his 'colleague in America' and refusing to divulge his name. He'd phoned Barbara Somersby and been absolutely truthful with her, and after some hesitation she'd given him the name of Dr Sam Wiseman. She thought he lived in New York.

There were thousands of Wisemans in the US Medical Directory, hundreds of Samuel Wisemans, nearly forty of them in the Big Apple. He'd systematically phoned each of them and it wasn't until he'd reached number

116

thirty-one that the suggestion was made that he might mean Dr Sam Weisman.

Bingo.

Weisman's tone became a good deal friendlier when Fraser mentioned JS, and he agreed to meet him.

'You don't realise just how vast America is till you go there,' he told Marcus. 'I flew, of course, but it still took the whole weekend for a couple of hours' chat with him.'

Weisman, a small, simian-featured man of around fifty, had been suspicious at first, JS notwithstanding, but when Fraser told him his story, he relaxed.

'I guess I was one of the first, if not *the* first, to trial Alkovin and I found pretty much the same as you,' he told him. 'Definitely improved remission induction, ninety-five per cent plus I'd guess, but then problems with psychosis after first consolidation.'

'In what percentage of patients?' Fraser asked.

'Forty-five, fifty.'

Fraser nodded. 'Sounds familiar. Any suicides?'

'Six attempted, two successful.'

'How many patients?'

'Around a hundred fifty.'

So why hadn't he published? Fraser asked.

He had, or leastways, he'd tried. The

117

journal he'd chosen had accepted his paper, but with the proviso that the report of psychosis was deleted. 'They said it was contentious, subjective, that I wasn't a psychiatrist, and that if it existed at all it was to do with the neighbourhood I worked with.' He made an indescribable noise with his lips that Fraser took to express scorn. 'I told 'em where they could shove it.'

He'd tried several other journals with the same result.

'Was it nobbled?' Fraser asked.

Weisman shrugged. 'Guess it must have been. Always knew there was a network of the high 'n' mighty out there — never imagined it was that powerful, though.'

Eventually it had been accepted by a little-known periodical.

'The trouble is,' Fraser told Marcus now, 'that there're papers raving about Alkovin, and Weisman's, when it comes out, will be ignored as a freak.'

'So what exactly are you suggesting, Dr Callan?' Marcus asked. 'Why have you come to us?'

'There's a problem with that drug that my bosses are pretending doesn't exist. Why, I don't know, but meanwhile, patients, including my fiancée, are suffering.'

'Are you suggesting that they've got some

118

interest in the drug company?'

Fraser hesitated. 'As I said, I don't know. But I do think it bears looking into.'

Marcus nodded slowly and turned to the man beside him. 'Any questions, Tom?'

So far, Tom Jones had said very little, although his gaze had hardly left Fraser's face, as though he was analysing every word he said.

'Dr Callan . . . ' The same distinct London accent he'd heard over the phone. 'You told us earlier about the murder of your previous director, Dr Somersby. D'you think that was part of this scenario?' He was the complete antithesis of Marcus Evans — leather jacket, rather loud tie and a disconcerting, even menacing air.

'I did wonder about it,' Fraser said after a pause. Then: 'The police questioned everyone concerned pretty rigorously . . . '

'Did they question you?'

'Aye, they did.'

'Rigorously?'

'Not what I'd call rigorously, but I had no motive for killing him. I *liked* the man.'

'So, who *did* have a motive?'

'I suppose the obvious ones were Connie, Ian Saunders and Leo Farleigh.'

'Because they wanted the drug trial and Dr Somersby didn't?'

119

'That's right. Connie and Ian might have wanted his job, although neither of them could have been sure of getting it.'

* * *

'What do you think, Tom?' Marcus asked after Fraser had gone.

After a pause, Tom said, 'We have to remember that we've only heard Callan's version. It could be that he's simply being vindictive, trying to make trouble for his boss because she had him suspended.'

'What's your gut feeling?'

'By and large, that he's straight.' Tom paused again. 'It smells, and it's not the first time we've come across Parc-Reed, is it? The anti-AIDS drug in Oxford — remember?'

'Yes, I do, now you come to mention it . . .'

Tom got up. 'The first thing is to check how they're doing on the stock market, and then whether any of the people Callan named hold shares.'

He was back after half an hour.

'Parc-Reed shares have doubled since they announced Alkovin and are still going up.'

'Interesting.'

'Yes. The drug's about to be launched on the open market and I'm told the shares

120

could double again.'

'Do any of Callan's friends have any?'

'Leo Farleigh holds a couple of thousand, but all the employees were given those when they went public. Neither of the others have any registered under their names.'

'What about *not* under their names?'

'That's just it — there's nothing to have stopped them setting up nominee accounts . . . ' Anybody, he explained, could go to a stockbroker anywhere in the country and set up a nominee account, so that only the broker's name appeared on the register.

'And that's almost certainly what they would have done.'

'Can you trace them?'

'I don't know. They'd have used a broker away from home . . . I'll look into it.'

10

A couple of days later, on Saturday, Frances said she wanted to drive over to see her mother on her own.

Fraser looked at her. 'Are you sure you're ready for that?'

'I've been on the Smarties for over a week now and I'm feeling much better.'

It was true — her moods, which had veered every which way for most of the week, seemed to have settled.

'Fraser,' she said, 'I've got to go back into hospital on Monday and I need some independence, some space.'

'All right,' he said. 'But if you feel an attack coming on — '

'I'll take the mobile and I'll stop and ring you. Promise.'

She put her hands on his shoulders, kissed the side of his mouth and the tip of his nose before going upstairs to get ready.

It was probably as well, he thought after she'd gone: the last week had been a strain for both of them. He'd taken her out as much as possible, but three times she'd asked him to stop the car and then just cried while he held her. That, he didn't mind so much. It was her suddenly screaming and throwing a saucepan out of the kitchen window without opening it first he found difficult to handle . . .

He prowled the house awhile, wondering what to do — suspension could get seriously boring, he thought. How long would it take Marcus Evans to get something going?

The phone rang — *Frances* . . . ? He snatched it up.

'Hello?'

'Fraser, it's Connie — please don't hang up . . . '

He'd almost dropped the receiver when he'd heard her voice.

'If we go on like we have been,' she said, 'we're going to do each other a lot of damage.'

'That's true,' he said non-committally as he thought, *She's been talking to the BMA*.

'I've been thinking things over,' she said slowly, obviously having difficulty enunciating her thoughts. 'I've been looking at your data and . . . the fact is, I've been wondering if you might be right about Alkovin.' The last came out in a rush.

'Well, that's good news,' said Fraser, at a loss to know what else to say.

'If you'll come over to my house now, we'll work out what to do about it.'

Fraser's mind was in a whirl. He could hardly tell her that he'd already put Marcus Evans on to her . . . but the last thing Evans had said to him was to act naturally.

'All right, Connie. I can be with you in . . . half an hour?'

'Sooner if you can, please, Fraser. I'm worried about the others.'

'All right,' he said.

Others? he wondered as he put the phone down. Ian and Leo? He glanced at his watch — Frances wouldn't have arrived at her mother's yet, better give it a bit longer.

He showered, changed, then rang Mary.

'No, not yet, dear,' she said, then: 'Wait, that's her car now, d'you want to speak to her?'

'No, she'll think I don't trust her. 'Bye.' He put the phone down, then compressed his lips together in thought for a moment before going out to his own car.

Connie lived about two or three miles away. She'd kept the house after her husband had left her, a mock Tudor edifice, rather pretentious, Fraser thought. It was set well back from the road in Avon's stockbroker belt. He was there within fifteen minutes.

He parked in the gravelled drive and walked over to the door. His shirt was sticking to him: the sun was more or less directly overhead and the leaves on the surrounding trees were still.

On the steps lay a walking-stick. He picked it up and rang the bell.

No answer.

He rang again, then, noticing that the door was ajar, pushed it open.

'Connie,' he shouted. 'It's me, Fraser . . . '

★ ★ ★

She was lying on her side on the chequer-tiled hall floor and he was kneeling beside her, although he couldn't remember doing so or how long he'd been there . . .

She had no pulse, although she was still warm. The back of her head was sticky and there was a small pool of blood he hadn't noticed before, perhaps because it was on a black tile . . . and a puddle of urine he hadn't noticed either.

And a noise behind him. He spun round on his haunches to find Leo Farleigh staring down at him. He hadn't heard his car . . .

Fraser said, 'She's dead . . . We'd better phone the police.'

'Yeah.' Leo said, 'sure . . . I'll do it now, shall I?'

'Aye, if you like.'

Leo edged past him and vanished into the

gloom of the house. Fraser found himself looking at the stick, now lying on the tiled floor . . . the heavy knobbed end was bloody, he hadn't noticed that before . . . it must be the murder weapon . . .

His head snapped up to where Leo had gone. *He thinks I did it* . . . No wonder he'd slunk past him so carefully . . .

He stood up, his head swam and he reached out for the wall to steady himself for a moment.

'Leo,' he called. 'Leo, have you phoned them yet?'

'Yeah,' came muffled from inside. 'They're on their way.'

Fraser walked into the room, peered, saw Leo over by the desk. 'Ah, there you are. I found her like that, not two minutes before you arrived. She phoned me, asked me to come over.' He was gabbling, he realised. 'Did she phone you, too?'

'Er, yeah, that's right.'

'When?'

'Oh, about an hour ago — I'm not sure.'

Fraser was pondering whether to ask him what the call was about when they heard the police siren.

★ ★ ★

There were two of them, a man and a woman, in a panda car. Fraser told them what had happened. He asked if he could wash his hands and was told No, not until the Scene of Crime staff had taken swabs from them.

'Oh, it's her blood,' he said. 'I was seeing if there was anything I could do for her.'

Nevertheless, they told him, they'd better stick by the book.

Inspector Lyn Harvey and a sergeant arrived, followed almost immediately by the SOC team. Fraser, who was beginning to feel as though his hands were contaminated, asked if they could be swabbed so that he could wash them.

This was done, and then he repeated his story. Leo was saying very little, he noticed.

Lyn Harvey said, 'I think we'd better get you both down to the station to make statements.'

'What about my car?' Fraser asked.

'We'll bring you back,' Lyn told him.

They drove to the police station in silence, Fraser and Leo both in the back of the car. Fraser was taken to a small room by Lyn, who, after offering him tea, began questioning him. He explained how Connie had phoned, how he'd driven to her house and found the stick.

'What made you pick it up, sir?' Lyn asked. 'The stick.'

'It was there lying on the steps, I assumed it had been dropped.'

'You didn't notice the blood on it?'

'Not at the time, no.'

Lyn didn't say anything and Fraser felt impelled to continue. 'I had no reason to look for it, I suppose. No reason to think it was there.'

When Fraser had finished telling her about finding Connie's body and Leo's arrival, Lyn asked him about his relationship with Connie.

'To be perfectly honest, Inspector, it wasn't very good.'

'Why was that, sir?'

Fraser told her about Alkovin and how he'd been suspended.

'So when you say your relationship wasn't very good, sir, what you really mean is that it was about as bad as it could be?'

'Yes, but I think that might have been about to change.' He gave her the gist of Connie's phone call.

Lyn looked at him reflectively for a moment.

'Who were these 'others' that Dr Flint referred to, sir?'

'I don't know. She didn't say.'

'Who do you *think* they were?'

Fraser hesitated, saw no way of avoiding it and named Leo and Ian.

'So what you're saying is that Dr Saunders and Mr Farleigh probably weren't on good terms with Dr Flint either?'

'That would depend on whether or not they knew she'd changed her mind about Alkovin, Inspector.'

'I see,' said Lyn after another pause.

They went through everything again, then Lyn wrote it down in the form of a statement, which Fraser read through before signing every page. Then, after he'd been told not to leave the area without telling the police first, a constable was found to take him back to his car.

He felt utterly drained and had no sense of time whatsoever — it seemed both minutes and days since he'd last seen the driveway and Connie's house. The area round the door had been cordoned off and people were still working there. Fraser didn't know whether Connie's body had been removed, although he assumed it had.

It wasn't until he was driving home that he remembered that Frances was with Mary. He rang her number as soon as he got back. Mary answered.

'Fraser, where have you been?'

'Is Frances OK?'

'She's tired and doesn't want to drive back. We've been trying to phone you, but she's thinking now she might as well stay here the night.'

'Is she actually with you now?'

'Er — she's in the living-room at the moment.'

'Listen, Mary . . . ' He quickly told her what had happened. 'I don't think it would be a good idea for Frances to know about it, not yet.'

'I think you're right, Fraser.'

'I'll come and pick her up tomorrow morning.'

Mary called Frances over to the phone. She asked him what he had been doing and he improvised, quite imaginatively, he thought.

'Have you got your Smarties there with you?' he asked.

'Yes — don't worry, I won't forget to take them. I don't want to go back there again,' she added in a small voice.

'How are you feeling now?'

'A bit washed out, otherwise OK. Looking forward to seeing you tomorrow.'

'Sure. Love you.'

'Love you too.'

He cooked himself a meal which he couldn't finish. He mowed the lawn, tried to tidy up the garden. His nerves were fired up with static and he couldn't settle to anything.

There was a goodish film on TV which killed a couple of hours, but after that, nothing, so he tried to read a book. It was then that he realised he should have rung Marcus Evans at home to tell him what had happened. Too late now, do it tomorrow.

He was certain he wouldn't be able to sleep, but felt guilty about drinking, since he'd been doing so much lately. Sure enough, as soon as his eyes were closed, images of Connie's face with wide open eyes paraded through his mind . . . and the pool of blood and the somehow pathetic puddle of urine.

So, who . . . ?

Ian? Leo?

He'd have thought Leo the most likely, but for the fact that he'd arrived after Fraser — His eyes snapped open in the dark. *But who was to say that he hadn't been there before, as well?*

He got out of bed, padded downstairs and found pen and paper, also a glass, which he filled with whisky — there'd be no sleep unless he had something.

He started writing down everything he could remember about Leo and Alkovin, about Leo's demeanour when he'd turned up so fortuitously at Connie's. He topped up his glass.

It was after two when he went back to bed. He fell into a dream in which Connie pursued him, telling him that it was all Frances' fault, until at last she screamed at him and he awoke to the strident chirrup of the phone.

'Hello . . . '

'Fraser, it's Mary.' Her voice was shot with panic. 'Frances is having some kind of fit. What shall I *do*?'

'Describe it.'

'She started screaming, then she smashed a cereal bowl on the floor, now she's lying on the sofa, crying.'

· Fraser tried to think . . . 'It's probably best if I come over, I'll be there as soon as I can.'

'All right, but *please* hurry . . . '

He banged the phone down and swung out of bed — and immediately toppled on to the floor.

His head alternately throbbed and spun . . . He heaved in some deep breaths, then slowly pushed himself up again . . . A bit shaky, not too bad. He pulled on some clothes, made for the loo. Perhaps he should have told her to phone Dr Parker . . . No — quicker if he went.

Had to have some coffee . . . He went

downstairs, put on the kettle — *Shit*! What if he was still over the drink drive limit?

Too bad.

He chewed up some paracetamol, then slopped some hottish water on to the coffee granules and swallowed down the resulting slurry. Opened the door, sucked in a few more deep breaths before unlocking the garage.

The MG started immediately and he left it running while he closed the garage. Turned to find a police car pulling up in front. His aching head smouldered as two men climbed out and approached him.

'Dr Callan?'

'Yes, but I'm afraid I can't stop — '

'We've come to take you down to the station, sir.'

'It'll have to wait, my fiancée's ill and I have to go and — '

'This isn't a request, sir.'

'She's *ill*, dammit — I'm sorry, but you'll have to — '

One of them gripped his arm. 'Please don't make this — *hweeeer* . . . '

His breath wheezed out as Fraser's elbow jabbed into his belly and he fell back clutching it. The other lunged at him, but his chin somehow ran into Fraser's fist. Fraser pushed him over and leapt into his car, gunned the engine, ploughed through his neighbour's lawn and away.

Oh shit shit shit what have I done . . . ?

He put his foot down.

For insurance purposes, the MGB is classified as a sports car, but other than for its road holding, it has no advantage over an average family saloon, let alone a police car. Two of them cut him off a mile from Mary's house.

He got out and stood still as they cuffed his hands behind his back and bundled him into one of the cars. As they set off, he said quietly but firmly to the plainclothes man next to him, 'I'm sorry for the trouble I've caused, but will you please phone my GP and ask him to go and see my fiancée? She's very ill.'

The plainclothes man said after a pause, 'And where is your fiancée?'

'At 22, Laurel Gardens. I was trying to get to her. Please, she's very ill.'

The man stared at him a moment before putting the call through to the station.

11

They left him in a room with a police constable and an equally silent cup of machine coffee, all part of the softening up process, he assumed. After about half an hour, he demanded to know what was being done about Frances. The constable passed the question on and the answer came back that Dr Parker had been called. Fraser had already been asked if he wanted legal advice and had spoken to the only firm of solicitors he knew, the one that had handled his house conveyance.

After another thirty minutes or so, the door opened and Lyn Harvey came in, accompanied by a tall, rather good-looking woman of about Fraser's age.

'Your GP, Dr Parker, has seen your fiancée and says to tell you that there's nothing to worry about.'

'Thank you,' said Fraser.

'This is Mrs Croft, the solicitor you requested.'

'Agnes Croft.' She held out her hand to Fraser. It was cool and soft. She turned to Lyn. 'Perhaps we could be left alone, Inspector.'

Over the next two hours, she took notes and asked questions while Fraser told her everything he could think of, up to his *faux pas* that morning.

'I've been kicking myself ever since,' he said.

'And so you should,' she said. 'Striking a police officer is just about the worst crime there is in their book — and it's given them more authority over you than they'd have otherwise had.' She sighed. 'Oh well, from the sound of things, they were going to arrest you anyway. Let's find out what they've got.' She stood up. 'Remember, pause before you answer each question in case I tell you not to answer it.'

They were taken down to a windowless room with recording equipment on a table against the wall. Fraser sat with Lyn Harvey opposite him and a tall, soldierly man with a moustache adjacent to them both. Agnes Croft sat as near as she could to Fraser.

Lyn tested the equipment, then named those present. The tall man was Superintendent Garrett.

'Dr Callan, you told me yesterday that your relationship with Dr Flint — and I quote — 'wasn't very good'. That was something of an understatement, wasn't it?'

Fraser said after a pause, 'As a professional

person, that was how I saw it and wished to describe it.'

'I see. Could you tell us how, and why, your relationship with her came to deteriorate so much — over the last two years, shall we say? As you saw it,' she added, with the merest touch of irony.

Once again, Fraser described his dispute with Connie over Alkovin, trying to present it as dispassionately as possible.

'So in effect,' Lyn said when he'd finished, 'she exiled you to America for three months?'

'If you care to put it like that, yes. It turned out to be quite a useful experience,' he added.

'One witness has told us that Dr Flint described it as a cooling-off period, your last chance, and gave you the option of accepting it or facing dismissal.'

Thanks, Ian . . .

'Well, Dr Callan?'

'In essence, that's true.'

'This witness also said that a state of open warfare existed between you and Dr Flint.'

'That is an exaggeration.'

'Is it? The people we've spoken to at your workplace all agree that the relationship between you was appalling.'

'As I told you yesterday, it wasn't very good. Open warfare is an exaggeration.'

After a slight pause, Lyn continued, 'You

returned from America on Friday, 7th May to discover that your fiancée, Frances Templeton, had leukaemia and was being treated by Dr Flint?'

'Yes.'

'It must have come as a shock?'

'Yes, it did.'

'Your fiancée knew about her condition several days before your return, and yet she chose not to tell you about it. Why was that, d'you think?'

Agnes came in quickly. 'Don't answer that for the moment, Fraser.'

Lyn continued as though the interruption hadn't taken place. 'You're very worried about your fiancée, aren't you, Dr Callan?'

'You know I am. She's now suffering from clinical depression and her mother phoned me this morning to tell me she was having a fit — that's why I tried to get away from your officers.' He thought he might as well get it in while he could.

'You must have been horrified when you discovered on your return that Dr Flint was treating her with Alkovin?'

'I wasn't pleased.'

'More understatement?'

Fraser didn't reply and Lyn went on, 'On Saturday, 8th May, after visiting your fiancée in hospital, you went to see Dr Flint in her office, didn't you?'

'Yes.'

'Where you threatened her.'

'I did not.'

'You didn't threaten her?'

'No.'

'We have a witness who overheard your conversation with her.' She extracted a sheet of paper and read from it . . . 'Dr Flint said, 'Are you threatening me, Fraser?' and Dr Callan answered, 'Yes, I am threatening you.' '

Thank you, Terry, Fraser thought, then said, 'That has been taken out of context.'

'Really? The statement continues: Dr Flint said, 'All you have to threaten me with is violence,' and then, 'Would you kill me, Fraser?' Dr Callan replied, 'If anything happened to Frances, then I would kill you.' ' Lyn looked up. 'And something *did* happen to Frances, didn't it? The very thing you'd feared — she developed clinical depression. Didn't she, Dr Callan?'

Agnes said, 'We seem to be straying into rather esoteric areas. I request a break to talk with my client.'

Garrett said, 'You had plenty of time to talk to your client earlier, Mrs Croft. We've been going for less than an hour and I think we should hear Dr Callan's answer to DI

Harvey's question. We'll break before long.'

Lyn said, 'Frances developed clinical depression, didn't she, Dr Callan?'

'Yes.'

'You must have found it very upsetting?'

'Of course I did.'

'And it made you angry?'

Fraser glanced at Agnes, who nodded. He said, 'Yes, it did.'

'And on Friday, 2nd July, after Frances had been diagnosed with clinical depression, you went and — er — had it out with Dr Flint?'

'I conveyed my feelings to her, yes.'

'A witness describes hearing a scream from Dr Flint's room and the words 'Help, he's assaulting me,' and upon investigation, found her in a distraught state. She had bruising to the wrists, while you had slap marks on both sides of your face.'

'She did slap me,' said Fraser, 'which is why I held her wrists — to prevent her doing it again.'

'Why did she slap you, Dr Callan?'

Another nod from Agnes.

'She told me I needed counselling because of my relationship with Frances and I told her that she was in no position to judge other people's relationships.'

Lyn said disbelievingly, 'She slapped you for that?'

'Yes.' He didn't add that she'd also kneed his balls.

'I see. So then she accused you of assault and called in the police, since when you've been suspended pending enquiry?'

'That's true, but — '

'Effectively, that's the end of your career, isn't it, Dr Callan? I think we'll take a break now,' she said before Fraser could reply.

* ★ ★

'She's twisting everything around to make it look as bad as possible.'

'Of course she is,' Agnes said. 'That's her job. The advantage from our point of view is that it tells us what kind of case they're trying to build. Tell me again about the so-called threat you made to Dr Flint — everything you can remember.'

Fraser did so. Agnes continued:

'This man Stroud, does he have any grudge against you?'

'He might have,' Fraser said, and told her how JS had asked him to look into the laboratory and how he'd then seriously considered retiring Terry. 'I can't swear that Terry knew about it, but I'm as sure as I can be that he did.'

'All right. Now tell me again about the last

141

row, the so-called assault.'

Once again, Fraser did so.

'I think you were right not to mention the knee to the groin,' Agnes said. 'Forget it for now.' She glanced at her watch. 'Let's see what Act Two brings.'

★　★　★

This time, Garrett opened the questioning, asking Fraser to describe again the events after Connie had phoned him. His voice was surprisingly soft and, to Fraser, the more menacing for that.

After he'd finished, Garrett said, 'The stick you found on the steps — was it lying across the steps, or flat on one of them?'

Fraser thought. 'Flat, I think.'

'What made you pick it up?'

'It looked untidy, I assumed someone had dropped it.'

'And you noticed nothing strange about it?'

'Not at the time, no.'

'The knobbed end was quite heavily bloodstained.'

'Yes, I realised that later, but I didn't notice it at the time.'

'You told us how you pushed the door open — is that something you usually do when calling on people?'

'No, but there was no reply to my ringing and I noticed it was ajar, so I — '

'A lot ajar, or a little?'

'A little. I pushed it open and — '

'Still holding the stick?'

'Yes. I called out and then saw Dr Flint lying there . . . '

'What did you do with the stick then?'

'I — I put it down when I tried to see if there was anything I could do for her.'

'Put it down where?'

'On the floor . . . '

'You don't sound very sure about that.'

'I was more concerned about Dr Flint than the stick.'

'You see, Dr Callan, Mr Farleigh has told us that you were still holding the stick when he found you with Dr Flint's — '

'Then he's a bloody liar!' Fraser shouted.

Agnes leaned forward, touched his arm in warning. He swallowed, said, 'I want to tell you something about Leo Farleigh, Superintendent — if anyone killed Connie, then it was him, he had a lot more motive than me.'

'Tell us about Mr Farleigh's motive, Dr Callan.'

Fraser, knowing he hadn't introduced the subject at the best time or in the best way, glanced at Agnes again before telling them about Connie's call to him, how she'd said

143

she was worried about the 'others' . . . 'She could only have meant Leo and Ian Saunders, that they'd have tried to prevent her changing her mind about Alkovin.'

'How could they have known she'd changed her mind?'

'She must have told them — I asked Leo when he arrived if she'd phoned him and he said yes.'

'He'd just found you crouched beside a dead body with a stick in your hand, Dr Callan. He wasn't going to disagree with you about anything.'

'Are you saying she *didn't* phone him?'

'BT have a record of her call to you, but no record of her calling Mr Farleigh.'

'Well, if you know she called me, then why — '

'We know she *called* you, but not what she said. We have only your word for that, Dr Callan.'

There was a silence while Fraser absorbed this, then Garrett said, 'Let's get back to Mr Farleigh for a moment, doctor. I believe you had an — er — altercation with him quite recently, on Tuesday, 15th June, in fact?'

'We had words, yes.'

'He says you nearly throttled him when he tried to commiserate with you about Miss Templeton.'

144

Fraser took a breath and told him what had happened. 'He was trying to score points, Superintendent, that's why I lost my temper. It was wrong of me, I know, but I was short of sleep.'

Garrett said deliberately, 'PC Booker, one of the officers who tried to arrest you this morning, is in hospital with a suspected fractured jaw — is that because you were short of sleep as well?'

Fraser closed his eyes for a moment. 'I'm truly sorry to hear that, Superintendent, but you know how, and why, it happened.'

'Indeed I do, Dr Callan. The point is, though, that since your fiancée developed leukaemia, you seem to have developed a rather short fuse.' Barely pausing, he said, 'You and Dr Flint had a sexual relationship, didn't you?'

Fraser said, 'That was over two years ago — ' at the same time Agnes said, 'Don't answer that.'

Garrett continued as though she hadn't spoken. 'Even so, it does go some way to explaining the intensity of the hatred between you, doesn't it?'

'Don't answer, Fraser.'

Garrett leaned forward and spoke softly. 'I don't think you're a murderer, Dr Callan.'

Fraser looked up at him.

145

'I think you're a man under great stress. Your fiancée's dangerously ill, your career's in ruins. There but for fortune — who knows what any of us would do under those circumstances . . . ?'

Fraser gazed back at him, mesmerised, like a bird by a snake.

'We know that Dr Flint phoned you. Perhaps she did offer some sort of olive branch, asked you to come over and talk about it. Perhaps she then made it clear she still expected your capitulation, and in the heat of the moment, you grabbed the stick . . . didn't realise what you were doing. That wouldn't be murder, Dr Callan, not in my book. We're human, we all know about human frailty . . . '

Fraser closed his eyes and shook his head slightly, as though to clear it, then looked at Agnes. She looked back without expression, as though wanting to know the truth herself.

He said firmly, 'That is not what happened.'

★   ★   ★

They questioned him through the afternoon and charged him with Connie's murder in the evening.

'Will I get bail?' he asked Agnes afterwards.

146

'I'll try, of course,' she said. 'But the fact that you fractured a constabularial jaw isn't going to help. Don't hold out too much hope.'

Fraser pressed his lips together. 'Where will they send me?'

'Here or Shepton Mallet, maybe Gloucester. It shouldn't be too bad, you'll probably get a cell to yourself.'

When Frances came, they just held each other without speaking.

At last, Fraser said softly, 'How're you feeling, hen?'

'All right in myself. Otherwise pretty bloody.' She held him at arm's length. She looked drawn, but composed. 'How about you?'

'Pretty much the same. I didn't do it, Frances.'

'I know that,' she said, but it seemed to him that she said it a microsecond too late.

'I didn't,' he said again.

'I know. Where are they . . . where are you going to be?'

'I don't know yet. Shouldn't be too far away. I'll phone every day. And write.'

She tried to smile. 'And I'll come and see you every day as soon as this round of treatment's over.'

12

'He's guilty,' said Garrett. 'I wouldn't have charged him otherwise.'

'The evidence you've shown me is all circumstantial,' observed Tom.

' 'Some circumstantial evidence is very strong,' ' quoted Garrett, ' 'such as when you find a trout in the milk.' That was Henry David Thoreau in 1850, and it remains as valid today as it was then.'

'Mm,' said Tom, who'd heard the quotation before and was unimpressed. 'None of the evidence here strikes me as being quite so substantial as a trout.'

It was Monday afternoon and Fraser was still in custody at the police station. At his request, Agnes had told Marcus what had happened, and Garrett had given Tom permission to come and see Fraser so long as he spoke to Garrett first.

'Oh, come on,' he said now. 'Look at the weight of it — Callan has a nasty, bitter, ongoing row with Dr Flint for over a year and she sends him on sabbatical as a warning. On the day he comes back, he's heard threatening to kill her if his fiancée gets depressed, which in the circumstances of her illness is quite likely. Sure enough, a couple of months later, she *does* get depressed and the next day, Callan is suspended from duty for assaulting Dr Flint — '

'Suspended pending enquiry,' interrupted Tom.

'At the very least, he manhandled her, and whatever the outcome of the enquiry, he hadn't got much of a career left. Then, two days ago, he's found kneeling over her body with the murder weapon in his hand. His fingerprints are in the right place for striking the blow and he's covered in her blood. What more do you want?'

'If that's a serious question,' Tom said, 'I'd want either a witness who actually saw him do it, or some solid forensic evidence. Hasn't the lab come up with anything yet? Surely, if he'd hit her with that stick hard enough to kill her, there'd be microdots of blood on his clothes.'

'There *was* blood on his clothes.'

'Microdots?'

'Forensic haven't finished their investigations yet,' Garrett said carefully. 'Besides, microdots aren't inevitable.'

Tom said, 'None of the evidence you've shown me actually disproves his story.'

Garrett snorted. 'But it's so tenuous, who

else could have killed her in the time? Oh, don't tell me — Farleigh, who wasn't even there. I've never heard a more obvious attempt to shift the blame.'

Tom thought for a moment ... The evidence against Fraser *was* strong, but whether it was strong enough to convince a jury was debatable.

'I'd have thought you needed a bit more before going to court,' he said.

'And I think you underestimate the strength of our witnesses,' Garrett said a little more quietly. 'Especially Farleigh.'

'Who Callan says did it.'

Garrett continued as though Tom hadn't spoken: 'There's all the difference in the world between kneeling beside a body you've just found, and kneeling beside one you've just murdered. Farleigh convinces me it's the latter because of his observation that the stick was still in Callan's hand.'

It was a valid point, Tom conceded. He said, 'How sure are you that Farleigh's telling the truth?'

'Sure enough. He's very positive about it.'

Tom said slowly, thinking aloud, 'If it *is* true, then I imagine you're thinking that Callan must have had another row with her, hit her spontaneously, and then knelt beside her aghast at what he'd done.'

150

'With the stick still in his hand,' Garrett said. 'I'd be more than happy to go along with that. Manslaughter, a *crime passionnel* — especially in view of their previous sexual relationship.'

Tom had been wondering when that would come up. To him, the sex angle was a red herring — or should that be trout?

Whichever it was, to a jury, sex might equate with guilt . . .

★   ★   ★

'I didn't do it, Mr Jones,' Fraser said quietly.

Tom had listened carefully while he'd told him how he'd found Connie's body, and then again gone over the events that had led up to it. 'I had no reason to kill her,' he said, 'She was coming round to my point of view.'

'Unfortunately, we only have your word for that.'

'Why else would she ring me?'

'To put more pressure on you, remind you who was treating your fiancée, perhaps?'

'That's not what she said on the phone.'

'Maybe she was hoping that a mixture of reason and threats would bring you round. Maybe she intended to seduce you.'

'Ach, not *that* again . . . I'm engaged and my fiancée is sick . . . '

'In her mind, that might have made you all the more susceptible.'

'Not a chance.'

'In which case, hell hath no fury. She slapped you — *again* — and you retaliated.'

Fraser shook his head. 'That's ridiculous — an' I think you know it.' He managed a smile. 'Y' can put your fishin' rod away now.'

Tom smiled back. 'It might not seem ridiculous to a jury,' he said. Then, 'Let's get back to the stick — are you sure you weren't holding it when Farleigh arrived?'

'Yes, I am sure.'

'Difficult to be that certain, I'd have thought, in the circumstances.'

'I dropped it on the floor,' Fraser said slowly. 'I mind looking at it, noticing the stain on the knob and realising it must be what she'd been hit with . . . '

'Yes,' said Tom, 'but hit minutes before, or seconds before?'

'The blood was dry.'

'How d'you know? Did you touch it?'

'No, I didn't touch it,' Fraser said wearily, 'it just looked dry.'

'OK,' Tom said. 'You come in through the door, you see the body — when did you drop the stick?'

After a pause, Fraser said, 'I can't remember exactly.'

'So when Farleigh came in, you might have still been holding it — '

'The stick *was* on the floor,' Fraser interrupted suddenly, 'because I realised it was bloody *after* he'd come in.'

'So he was standing there when you saw it and realised it was bloody?'

'No, he'd gone to phone the police by then . . . '

'So you could have dropped it after he came in?'

'No! I'm sure it was on the floor when he came in.'

'Did you hear him arrive?'

'N-no . . . '

'Was his car outside at that stage?'

'I think so — yes, I saw it when the police brought us down here.'

'Was it there when you arrived at the house?'

'No.'

'So he got there after you, and yet you say he killed her.'

'Listen, Mr Jones . . . ' Fraser took a breath, tried to gather himself together. 'Assume for a moment that I'm telling the truth, that Connie rang and told me she'd had second thoughts . . . I'd already told you and your boss that I thought there was some sort of corruption going on, that Connie and

153

Ian and Leo were deliberately suppressing the truth about Alkovin . . . so if Connie did change her mind, then both Leo and Ian would have a motive for killing her.'

'But how could they have known she'd changed her mind?'

'I asked Leo at the time if she'd phoned him and he said yes.'

'But he denied it later, said he was humouring you. And there's no record of any call to him.'

'He was *there*, on the spot — *why*? Something must have brought him there . . . '

'But he arrived *after* you.'

'That doesn't mean he wasn't there before, does it?'

Tom thought about this, said, 'Are you saying he was there all the time, or that he came back?'

'Either. He could have parked at the back earlier, then driven his car round, put it next to mine, then come in to *discover* me with Connie's body.'

'Wouldn't you have heard his car if he'd done that?'

'I didn't hear it anyway.'

'Starting a car tends to make more noise than just driving it.'

'From the back of the house? I don't know, maybe you're right, maybe he drove away after he'd killed her and then came back.'

'Why would he have done that?'

'I don't know . . . maybe he left something there — Yes! That would explain why he was so eager to phone the police, to get back into the house . . . I found him over by Connie's desk . . . '

'He'd have been eager to phone the police anyway if he'd just found you with a dead body,' said Tom.

'Ach, I don't know,' Fraser said, burying his face in his hands.

Tom stared at him, genuinely unsure of what to believe, then Fraser looked up again.

'It all hinges on Alkovin, doesn't it?' His face was animated, feverish almost. 'Would I have come to you in the first place if I didn't believe it was dangerous?'

'I'm sure you believe it is, but that doesn't necessarily make it true.'

'Ah for God's sake, Frances is the living proof of it — what more d'you want?'

'You're assuming cause and effect . . . '

'Yeah, that's right, I am — who's the feckin' doctor, you or me?' He closed his eyes for a moment, pressed his lips together. 'Sorry. Look, if you don't believe me, why don't you ring up Dr Weisman in New York? He'll tell you.'

Tom leaned forward and said softly, 'I will, but assuming he confirms what you say, doesn't *that* give you rather a good motive for killing Dr Flint?

Fraser let out a groan. 'I keep telling you, not if she'd changed her mind, not if she was coming round — I can see you don't believe me, but for the sake of justice, will you look into it? Give Leo Farleigh and Ian Saunders some of what you've been giving me and then see what you think.'

'All right,' said Tom, 'I'll do that.'

★　★　★

'Still got doubts?'

Garrett had asked Tom to come and see him again after he'd finished with Fraser.

'Yes, I have.'

Garrett nodded to himself as if this were no more than he'd expected. He said, 'When Callan came to see you last week, did he say anything about the previous director, Dr Somersby?'

'Yes, he did,' Tom said slowly. 'He was murdered too, wasn't he, about two years ago?' He looked at Garrett quizzically.

'That's two directors murdered in two years — what would you normally think about that?'

'You're not suggesting he did both of them?'

'Why not?'

'By all accounts he and Somersby liked each other . . . '

'By *his* account, mostly. It was my case,' he added, 'and I can't help thinking now that it's more likely that one person did both murders.'

'You didn't suspect him at the time though, did you?'

'No, more's the pity, we might have looked at his car. From Somersby's injuries, we thought it was a low slung car, and Callan has a sports car. We're looking at it now, although it's far too late for any direct evidence.'

'Who did you suspect at the time?'

Garrett shrugged. 'Farleigh, Saunders, Dr Flint herself — take your pick . . . ' He gave Tom a résumé of what they'd done and copies of the case notes.

★ ★ ★

Fraser hadn't cried since he was twelve. He'd seen a boy of thirteen cry when he was bullied and remembered how he'd never thereafter shaken off the sobriquet Blub. He'd trained himself not to cry under any circumstances.

Now, as he stared stony-faced at the cell wall, he had to exercise that will-power more than at any time he could remember.

So they thought he'd killed JS as well, did they? It just proved they were mad —

Or that I am . . .

As this thought went through his mind, something inside him shifted and he twitched violently.

What if they are right?

Was it possible to murder someone and then remember nothing about it?

No, no — the stick, I remember picking up the stick . . .

But he hadn't noticed the blood on the knob at the time, had he?

Because I just didn't notice it? Or because it wasn't there at that stage?

13

'No. I don't think he did it, Mr Jones.'

'Why not?'

Agnes Croft considered for a moment — not her opinion, but the words to describe it. It was the following morning and they were in her office.

'Because there's no direct evidence against him, because his story is plausible in itself and, finally, because I believe him as a person.'

'What if there were direct evidence?'

'Then I wouldn't be so inclined to believe him. Nor if his story or personality didn't ring true. It's because of all three criteria that I do.' She returned Tom's level gaze. 'You, I take it, don't believe him?'

'I'm honestly not sure what to believe. The evidence against him's pretty strong and the police aren't the complete fools the media like to make them out to be.'

'I know that . . . ' She hesitated. 'Although I do think that trying to pin Dr Somersby's murder on him is a piece of pure opportunism.'

'I think I'd agree with you there. Although

Garrett does have a point about the likelihood of there being just one murderer.'

'Exactly!' she said. 'And Fraser Callan didn't commit either of them.'

'So who did?'

'Isn't that your job, Mr Jones?'

'No, Mrs Croft, as a matter of fact it isn't my job. At the moment my only job is to ascertain whether there's any truth in Dr Callan's allegation of corruption.'

'Couldn't the two be connected?'

'Quite possibly.'

She said carefully, 'Mr Jones, I wonder if there might be some mutual advantage if we were to collaborate?'

Tom grinned at her. Agnes Croft had fair curly hair, blue-grey eyes and a face that managed to be both strong and pretty. 'I can't help feeling, Mrs Croft, that you would stand to gain more from that than me.'

'Not necessarily. I could persuade people like Frances and her mother to speak to you more freely than they would otherwise.'

'What about people like Leo Farleigh and Ian Saunders?'

'That might be more difficult,' she conceded.

Tom thought for a moment . . . It might not be a bad idea to have Callan's solicitor on tap . . .

'All right,' he said.

She held out her hand. It was cool and smooth and felt rather pleasant.

Now would be the best time for him to talk to Frances, she told him; she'd just gone back into hospital for her third course of drugs and they might not have started to affect her yet. She phoned the hospital and arranged for Tom to see her that afternoon.

'Be gentle with her, won't you?' she said, 'Remember she's ill.'

Tom said, 'You're taking this case very seriously, aren't you?'

'I suppose I am.'

'Why?'

'Because what's happened to those two people is not fair,' she said after a pause. 'I know you can't make life fair and nor should we even want to, but that's no reason to ignore its more grotesque anomalies.'

★   ★   ★

Frances was up and dressed in a summer frock. His first impression was of a plain but not unattractive face with very clear grey eyes that watched him intently as he approached her.

'Mr Jones?'

He nodded. 'Miss Templeton.'

'Won't you sit down?' She indicated another chair.

'Thank you.'

Close to, he could see that her skin was dry, almost papery, and that there were lines around her mouth and jowl that made her look older than her years.

She said, 'Agnes — Mrs Croft — told me that you might be able to help Fraser.' Her voice was low, clear, with a slight accent, a sort of citified West Country that he thought must be Avonian.

He said carefully, 'Assuming that what he told me was the truth, then I might.'

'It *is* the truth.'

'Then what I'm looking for might help him.'

'What exactly *are* you looking for?'

Tom explained, then said, 'If he's right about Alkovin, and even more to the point, about the corruption, then it could give others a motive for killing Dr Flint.'

Frances grimaced. 'Well, I'm the living proof he's right about Alkovin.'

Tom thought quickly, said, 'Did Fraser feel as strongly about it before he went to America?' It wasn't the direction he'd intended going, but it was on offer, so he took it.

'Oh, yes.'

'Then whatever made you agree to be treated with it? Didn't you believe him?'

'Oh, I believed him, but . . . ' She hesitated. 'But 'clinical depression' was just words to me then. Hearing about it and living it are two very different things.'

He started to say something but she overrode him. 'When Dr Flint diagnosed me, my one idea was to get cured. Her figures clearly showed that Alkovin produced better remission and I thought: What's a bit of depression compared with a better chance of living?' She sighed. 'I had no idea what clinical depression could be like.'

'Bad?'

She looked away, then back at him. 'It's like a black hole. Every atom of hope is sucked out of you, and no matter how often you tell yourself it's the drug doing it, you don't believe it.' Her words came faster. 'It gets so you believe that the people around you, even those who love you, they aren't just unsympathetic, they're actually *conniving* at your misery . . . it gets worse and worse and at last you snap and go out of control.' She swallowed. 'Fraser told me how I hit him, threw things at him, but I can't remember doing it.' She tried to smile, but it came out lop-sided.

Then she told him how it was the morning

after she'd been diagnosed that Fraser had gone to see Connie and they'd had the row that led to his suspension . . . 'It was she who hit him, you know, not the other way round.'

'He does seem to have made a habit of that recently,' observed Tom. 'Being hit by women, I mean.'

She smiled suddenly, brilliantly, and her face took on a radiance that astonished him.

Then it faded as she said, 'It's occurred to me since that she reacted like that because she knew deep inside that he was right. It makes her phone call to him plausible.'

'Are you still being treated with Alkovin?'

'Yes.'

'Why, for God's sake?'

'Because to change now might compromise my chances of a cure. I've been on Prozac for a couple of weeks and it's stopped the depression.'

'So why on earth didn't you take it earlier?'

'Because Dr Flint wouldn't allow it. She doesn't — didn't, that is — believe in prophylactic treatment.'

'I see,' said Tom. What he saw, more clearly than ever, were Fraser Callan's reasons for hating Flint. 'You mentioned the phone call just now, when Dr Flint asked Fraser round to her house, but you weren't actually there at the time, were you?'

'No, more's the pity.'

'Could you tell me about that day, from your point of view?'

'All right . . . ' She told him how she'd decided to drive to her mother's.

'What time did you leave?' he asked.

'I'm not sure, about half-past ten, I suppose.'

'How about arriving?'

'I think around eleven — does it matter?'

'I'm trying to get all the details of that day right in my head . . . ' What he really wanted to find out was why Callan hadn't made more effort to bring her back home after he'd been released by the police. 'What did you do, once you got to your mother's?'

She shrugged. 'Chatted, had lunch, then went out shopping. It was that that did for me.'

'But you still intended to go back home?'

'Yes, but I didn't feel up to driving by then. I rang Fraser but couldn't get any reply. It wasn't until the next day that I found out why,' she added.

'But he rang you, didn't he?'

'Yes.'

'So why didn't he come and collect you?'

'At the time, because it seemed simpler that way, although I realise now that it was because he didn't want me to find out about Connie — '

Of course not! But in what sense . . . ?

' — I suppose he didn't think he'd be able to hide it from me.'

'You didn't realise anything was wrong from the way he spoke on the phone?'

'No. But by that time, I felt so near to collapse I was happy to stay at Mum's . . . If only I'd known . . . '

'Can you remember the next day?'

She nodded, her face becoming pinched again. 'I remember waking up . . . I'd had a terrible dream and I felt awful. I remember having a row with Mum, and then nothing — until I woke up again and Dr Parker, our GP, was there.'

'When did you find out what had happened to Dr Flint?'

'Not till the day after.' She smiled again, wanly. 'Mum had Dr Parker tell me in case I threw another wobbly.'

'Did you?'

She shook her head. 'I haven't had one since. Dr Parker says it's the Prozac.'

'Good stuff, then?'

She nodded. 'And some.'

'Did it surprise you, Fraser hitting a policeman and making a run for it?'

'Of course it did. He's always been a bit

short-tempered, but I've never known him to be violent before.' She continued: 'In a funny kind of way, it's rather flattering. He did it for me.'

'It's made things a lot worse for him.'

'Oh, I know that — I did say in a funny kind of way.'

'You know that the police are wondering whether Fraser killed Dr Somersby as well?' said Tom, changing tack.

'There's no *as well* about it,' she said sharply. 'Besides, I've never heard anything so ridiculous in my life.'

'Why d'you say that?'

'Because they got on so well.'

'How d'you know?'

'It was obvious, you could see they had an affinity. This was before we started going out together,' she added.

'What about Dr Flint?' Tom asked. 'Did Fraser ever have any affinity with her?'

'I know they had a one night stand, if that's what you're getting at,' she said drily. Then she added, 'I think it had more effect on her than him.'

'In what way?'

She thought for a moment, then said, 'I think she still wanted him afterwards, and then realised that he didn't want her . . . I'm sure it's a factor in the whole business, why

167

she hated him so much, why she was so bloody-minded when he tried to tell her about Alkovin.'

'Her feelings were that obvious?'

'Oh no, they were always very correct in public, I don't think anyone else knew about the one night stand.'

'But it was generally known they disliked each other?'

'I wouldn't have said it was *generally* known . . . Terry Stroud certainly knew, and maybe some of the others.'

'He's the one who heard Fraser threatening to kill her?'

'He's exaggerating. Besides, it was just after Fraser came back from America and found I was ill.'

He took the opportunity to go over everything she knew about the dispute. It didn't differ significantly from Callan's account. Then he asked her to contact him if she remembered anything else, and got up to go.

'I hope you're feeling better soon,' he said, the words sounding limp and inadequate in his ears.

'Thanks.' He was half-way to the door when she said, 'What would really make me feel better is some good news about Fraser. You will try, won't you?'

★ ★ ★

At that moment, Fraser was on his way to gaol.

He was sitting handcuffed in a cubicle, one of eight cubicles in a large van belonging to Group Four, although he was the only prisoner. There was no window and nothing to look at, not even graffiti. From the steady roar of the engine, he guessed they were on a motorway.

His troubles, Agnes had explained to him the previous evening, had come at a bad time. The local prisons were even more over-crowded than usual and he was being sent to Her Majesty's Prison Ship *Derwent*, a converted car ferry moored off Portland Island. She told him she was looking for the best available counsel, and that Tom Jones was investigating the corruption angle. His mouth turned down at that and Agnes told him that Jones was probably the nearest thing they had to a friend at that moment. The aloneness he'd felt as she'd left was one of the worst moments.

The van ground on. His mind turned to Frances — she'd be into the third course of drugs by now and he wondered how she was feeling . . .

There was a click and he looked up to see

an eye peering at him through the spy hole. The sight of it, for the second it lasted, seemed to encapsulate his whole life.

At last they came to a stop he sensed was final. The cubicle door opened.

'Let's be 'avin' you then, sunshine.'

The back of the van was opened and he stumbled out, blinking in the sudden brilliance. A heavy, black chain link fence stood in front of him, about twenty feet high. Behind it and to the left was a massive structure, perhaps fifty feet high — was *that* a ship?

A prison officer emerged from a hut and, selecting a key from the huge bunch hanging from his belt, unlocked the gate. Fraser was led forward.

'Remand prisoner for delivery,' the Group Four flunkey said as he handed over some paperwork.

They passed through another gate, then another. Into a terrapin hut. He was signed for and his hands uncuffed. The flunkey left and he was told to sit down.

After a few moments, another prison officer came in and gestured to him. 'This way.'

Another gate and a long passage that he suddenly realised was the gangway to the ship, then yet another gate to be unlocked

— did that make five or six?

A reception area, clean, bright, windowless — he was told to strip. His clothes were searched and returned to him. He was told he could keep one spare set of clothes and some books, but his other possessions would be stored.

A senior officer called McIlroy gave him a book of rules and went through some of them with him. Fraser listened, but he was only half there; it was as though he'd been put into a faulty time machine and the other half was somewhere else.

' . . . and because of the present over-crowding, you'll be sharing a cell with two putative illegal immigrants — '

'*What?*' His other half returned with a bang. 'I was told I'd get a cell to myself.'

McIlroy looked up. 'I'm sorry, Dr Callan, but we are accommodating you in accordance with the regulations laid down for remand prisoners. Maybe in a week or two the situation will improve.'

'But . . . these illegal immigrants . . . who are they?'

'Romanians. They're good lads.'

'Romanians . . . ' He swallowed. 'I've heard about what goes on in prisons . . . What if they try to . . . ?'

McIlroy said stiffly, 'You'll find nothing of

that kind occurring in this prison.'

Oh, great ... that's a real feckin' comfort ...

He allowed himself to be led up a flight of stairs. On the landing, two men in brown prison clothes were cleaning the floor and looked up incuriously as he passed.

They stopped to pick up some bedding, then went up another flight, then another — how high was he going?

There was a smell, the smell of school, of bodies, the smell of institutionalised humanity.

A brightly lit corridor — everything was bright. They stopped at a door. The officer slid it aside and peered.

'Nobody in, your chance to make yourself at home.'

Fraser followed him inside. The cell was about eight feet by ten. There was a single bed on one side, twin bunk beds on the other.

'Looks like you've got the top bunk.' The officer tossed the bedding on to it. 'You make your bed while I fetch your toilet tackle.'

Fraser started to sink down on to the single bed before remembering it was someone else's. In a daze, he looked round the cell ... In one corner was a triangular table and a chair, beside it a small chest of drawers with a bowl and jug. Beside that, in the other corner, was a pale blue rectangular object with a white lid and he realised he was looking at a chemical lavatory.

There was a noise outside, then the door slid open and two men came in. They wore T-shirts and jeans. One had thick dark hair, stubble and deep brown eyes; the other was fair with blue eyes. They both stared at him.

14

He froze as they stood there staring; he'd realised he was going to have to say something when the fair one said carefully, 'Hi.'

'Hi,' Fraser responded warily.

'Hi,' said the dark one, appraising him.

The two of them looked at each other; the fair one said something in what Fraser assumed was Romanian, then turned back to him. 'You,' he pointed, 'in — here?'

Fraser nodded. 'Yes.'

The fair one pointed to himself. 'Ilie Groza,' he said, and held out his hand.

Fraser took it — it was rough and hard with a fierce grip.

'Fraser Callan,' he said.

'Fra-ser?'

He nodded.

The other one said, 'Petru Branesco,' as they repeated the handshaking ritual, then hauled a plastic pouch from his jeans, sat on the bed and rolled a cigarette. He offered the pouch to Fraser, who shook his head.

'No, thanks.'

Petru shrugged and handed the pouch to

Ilie. He waited for him to roll, then lit up for them both. The air filled with acrid smoke and Fraser hoped the air conditioning worked.

Ilie looked at Fraser again, then picked up a dictionary from the table and thumbed through it.

'You,' he said to Fraser, 'you — snare?'

Snare . . . ? He looked at the word Ilie was pointing to, and for the first time that day, smiled.

'Snore,' he said, and Ilie repeated it.

'I don't think so . . . ' Fraser said, then shrugged and shook his head.

'Petru,' said Ilie, pointing, 'him — snore. Bad.'

It was at this point that Fraser realised they probably weren't planning a raid on his virtue that night — then there was a noise from the door and the warder came in.

'You lads got to know each other all ready then? Good, saves me trying to introduce you.'

He handed Fraser a plastic bag with a string-pull neck. 'That's your kit — soap, flannel, toothbrush — and here's your card for the phone. It's gotta last you a week, so don't lose it. If you do, you'll have to pay for another. OK?'

He nodded to the other two and left. Petru

gave his retreating back a one-fingered salute.

'Bastard,' Ilie said, but not until he was well out of earshot. It was one word he didn't have to look up, Fraser reflected.

He was looking something up now, though. He pointed at himself and said, 'Mech-anic.' Then at Petru. 'Boulder.'

Fraser was wondering dimly whether this was a reference to Petru's bravery or to Peter the rock of the Church when Ilie mimed bricklaying.

'Ah, a builder.'

'*Da!* Yes. Bil-der.' He pointed at Fraser interrogatively. 'You?'

Fraser took the dictionary from him and looked up doctor, for which the Romanian word was — *doctor*.

'Doctor,' he said. 'Medic.'

The two Romanians looked at each other. Petru said something which Ilie answered in a sharp burst of Romanian. Petru shrugged again — it seemed to be his favourite gesture.

Fraser started making up his bed on the top bunk to cover the moment. The blankets were grey and rather coarse and the sheets looked like linen, although it was more likely to be rough cotton, he reflected. He hadn't made up an old-fashioned bed since he'd left home, and now it was especially awkward because he had to reach up and over to do it.

He'd just about finished when a fist pounded on the door and a mocking voice intoned, 'Dinner is served, gentlemen.'

The two Romanians obviously knew what this meant. They stubbed their cigarettes, got up and stuffed their baccy pouches into their jeans. Fraser wasn't hungry, but decided he might as well go with them.

In the corridor, it seemed as though the whole wing was on the move as prisoners streamed out of their cells, some in jeans, some in prison garb. Fraser went with the crowd, keeping close to Ilie and Petru. At the moment, they were the nearest thing he had to friends . . . discounting Jones, that is, he thought wryly.

They turned into a large dining area and joined a queue. Fraser looked round. He'd subconsciously expected long, schooltype benches, but instead there were ranks of tables and chairs for four. Ahead was an army-style canteen where men in chefs' hats served food across a stainless steel counter.

The queue shuffled slowly forward. Ilie and Petru picked up trays and plastic cutlery. On offer were fried fish, stew with dumplings, vegetable curry and rice, chips, baked potatoes and cabbage. The Romanians had stew and chips. Fraser took stew, potatoes and cabbage.

All the tables near the windows were taken. They sat at one near the middle of the room.

The stew was surprisingly good and Fraser had just realised how hungry he was when his shoulder was nudged, sharply. He looked round to see two big, swarthy men, one of whom indicated with a gesture of his head that he should move to another table. He hesitated, anger fighting with prudence . . .

'No,' Ilie said softly.

The other spoke quickly in Romanian. Petru answered, his voice hard. The other made a mouth and moved on.

Petru winked at Fraser, then pointed to his plate and said, 'Good.'

Fraser nodded and smiled as the thought struck him that this probably *was* better than anything they'd had in Romania.

When they'd finished, they took their trays to a stacking point, then Fraser followed them to a common room. It was thick with smoke and men crowded round a TV in one corner. A clock on the wall said it was nearly seven. Fraser touched Ilie's arm and mimed a phone.

'Ah, *telefon* . . . ' He pointed to the door and indicated right.

'Thanks.' He nodded to both of them, raised a hand and went out.

A warder gave him more directions and he

followed the corridor round to find a queue of about twenty people waiting for two phones.

Nothing for it, so he joined them.

He thought about his cell mates, their rapid talk in the cell when they realised he was a doctor, the way they'd moved their compatriots on in the canteen ... Maybe they thought he was worth cultivating, might be useful to them in some way ... He glanced down at the phonecard in his hand. It was for thirty units, that would never last a week, surely —

'Get a fucken move on,' a voice called. 'Yeah, you!'

A rodent-like man in prison garb said a few hurried words into the phone and hung up. The queue moved forward and Fraser reflected that maybe it might last the week after all ...

A quarter of an hour later, it was his turn. With shaking fingers, he pushed in the card and keyed in the numbers. Heard it ringing ... There was no privacy, not even the spurious comfort of a perspex shell, but at least the gum-chewing man behind him hung back a little.

'Frances ... ?' It was her voice. 'How are you, hen? How're you feeling?'

'I'm all right, darling — what about you? Is it awful?'

'I'll survive, I feel better already just for hearing you . . . ' He told her about Ilie and Petru and she told him about Tom's visit.

'At least he's doing something, Fraser.'

'Time's up, mate,' came a voice from behind him.

'Gotta go, love,' he said. 'Same time tomorrow, love you.'

'Love you too, Fraser . . . '

He walked away as the gum-chewing man took his place; her voice was still in his ears and he wanted to sink down somewhere with his face in his hands, but that was one thing you couldn't do here . . .

Keep moving, to loiter is to be conspicuous.

He clenched his teeth on his misery and kept moving.

A sign for a bog — might be worth trying to go now, avoid having to use that thing in the cell.

As he turned into it, the smells of ammonia, shit and disinfectant greeted his nostrils and —

Another feckin' queue . . .

He joined it. Shuffled slowly forward. A warder stood watching. He went into a cubicle and shut the door — half-door, rather. It shielded the top of the pan and his midriff from view, but not his feet or head.

He dropped his trousers and sat down. The seat was warm. A con shuffled past, not looking at him, but the invasion of this most basic of privacies made his guts seize up. He gave it a minute, then gave up.

'You'll get used to it, mate,' the screw said as he went past him over to the basin.

In the corridor, the screws were shouting for lock-up. Back in the cell, Petru lay on his bed, smoking and listening to a radio. Ilie looked up from his dictionary.

'Chest?' he said.

'Chest?' repeated Fraser, wondering for a moment if it could be an enquiry as to whether the smoke was bothering him.

Ilie pointed at the word in the dictionary — chess — then pointed at Fraser, 'You?'

'All right, Ilie,' he said with a smile. 'Why not?'

Ilie brought out a board and set the pieces with incredible speed, then gave Fraser white and indicated for him to start. Fraser absent-mindedly pushed a pawn forward two squares, his mind still full of Frances. About five minutes later, he realised he'd been mated.

'Bluidy hell!'

They started again and this time he tried to concentrate more and succeeded in delaying defeat for a quarter of an hour. Ilie's technique was simple: Blitzkrieg. He moved all his major pieces out immediately and commenced slaughter.

'Another,' Fraser said grimly.

This time, he thought out his strategy and the game lasted nearly an hour, although Ilie beat him in the end. They shook hands, grinning.

Lights out was at ten. Fraser self-consciously squirmed into his pyjamas, anxious for a moment lest his earlier optimism might be misplaced, but the Romanians ignored him. They slept naked, he noticed.

He thought he'd have difficulty sleeping and he was right. He lay between the rough sheets thinking about Frances, about Jones and the questions he might be asking. He thought about Leo, about how much he'd like half an hour alone with him to put a few questions of his own . . .

Petru began snoring. Ilie hadn't been kidding, it was like the foghorn he'd once heard off the Mull of Kintyre.

After a while, he got out of bed and, in the dim light of the security lamp, found some loo paper to chew up and use as ear plugs. He was just wondering whether or not to give Petru a shake when Ilie woke up, reached over and gave him a shove that knocked him a foot sideways. It didn't wake him, but the snoring stopped.

It started again a few minutes later, but the ear plugs muffled the sound enough for Fraser to drift into a state of semiconsciousness that eventually led to oblivion.

★　★　★

After he'd seen Frances, Tom rang Mary Templeton, who said he could come round to her house in an hour, so he decided to go and have a look at the scene of the murder. He found it in the A – Z, then, on impulse, drove to Fraser's house first.

It was a semi in a fairly modern estate and didn't have much character, unless you counted the still visible tyre slashes across the lawns and gardens where Fraser had done his runner.

Must have pleased the neighbours.

From there, he drove to Connie's, taking the route he assumed Fraser would have taken. It took him nearly twenty minutes, but he was sure it would be considerably less for someone who knew the way.

Connie Flint's house was in a wide, leafy suburb, and was several indices removed from Fraser's. He negotiated the drive and parked next to the SOC van that was there. A man came out of the house almost immediately and Tom showed him his ID.

'I'm surprised to find any of you lot still here,' he said.

'Just clearing up.'

'Did you hear me arriving from in there?' Tom asked.

'Your car does have rather a distinctive note,' the man said, nodding at the Cooper.

'Would you have heard a quieter car?'

'Couldn't tell you, mate.'

Tom told him he was going to have a look round and the man shrugged and said, 'Sure.'

He looked at the steps where Fraser said he'd found the stick and then at the chequered hall inside. The position of the body was still marked out.

'It's not as if there's anyone here to disturb,' the man said, as though to explain his tardiness.

Tom nodded, then went inside to look at the phone and desk that Callan had suggested Leo Farleigh was so interested in. Nothing there grabbed his attention, so he went outside and followed the gravelled drive round to the back of the house, where there was certainly plenty of room to park a car out of sight.

He returned slowly to the front.

'Do me a favour?' he asked the SOC man.

'Depends what it is.'

'Drive your van round to the back, switch off, then start up again and drive back.'

'Sure.'

Standing where the body had been with the door just ajar, Tom heard him start the engine, but nothing more until he reappeared again in the hall. He then asked him to reverse back down to the road, and return slowly to the house. The man agreed, but not quite so readily.

This time, Tom could just make out the crunch of tyres on gravel as he drew up. *But would I have heard it if I'd just found a body and wasn't listening for it . . . ?*

He thanked the SOC man and left. In the tree-lined street, he stopped.

A car wouldn't have to drive far along it to be out of sight, he thought, so it was possible for Leo to have left the house, Fraser to have arrived and Leo to have then returned, without them being aware of each other — although Leo would have known someone was there as soon as he saw Fraser's car . . . Wouldn't he have then driven off again? No, because for all he knew, he'd have been heard and/or seen arriving.

The same applied if he'd been parked round the back when Fraser arrived.

185

Whichever (if either), his only safe course would be to pretend that *he'd* only just arrived . . .

Witnesses? Tom looked up and down the street — most of the houses were out of sight and it wasn't the kind of neighbourhood with a lot of pedestrian traffic, so it wasn't altogether surprising the police hadn't found any.

He checked Mary Templeton's address again, found it on his A – Z and was there in ten minutes.

'Mr Jones? Do come in.'

She was a homely woman with a comfortable figure, a blue rinse and a face with a clear resemblance to Frances'. She had the same town-and-country accent, only more pronounced.

If you want to know how your wife'll turn out, Tom thought, paraphrasing Oscar, *all you have to do is look at her mother . . .*

She took him through to a rather pedestrian sitting-room and offered him tea, which he declined.

She sat down nervously on the edge of a chair, then, before Tom could say anything, said in a voice that trembled slightly, 'Mrs Croft told me you might be able to help Fraser.'

Tom suddenly saw a woman whose

daughter was gravely ill, and whose prospective son-in-law was charged with murder, and felt a flush of shame at his derogatory thoughts.

'The operative word is *might*,' he said gently.

'How can I help?' she said firmly.

'By telling me about last weekend,' Tom told her.

Her story tallied with the others. Frances had phoned her at about ten to make the arrangement, and Fraser had phoned at a little after eleven to ask if she had arrived. 'I told him she was just arriving and asked if he wanted to speak to her, but he didn't want her to think he was spying on her.'

They'd chatted, had lunch and, later, gone to the shops. When they'd got back, Frances had been too exhausted to drive and they'd tried to ring Fraser.

'We were just beginning to get worried when he called us.'

'Who actually answered the phone?' Tom asked.

'I did.'

'This is important, Mrs Templeton,' he said, leaning forward. 'What exactly did he say to you? As near as you can remember.'

'Well . . . ' She frowned as she thought. 'He asked how Frances was and I told him, then he asked if she was there beside me, and when I said no, he — he told me what had happened.'

'What had happened to Dr Flint, you mean?'

'Yes. I was very shocked, of course, and when he said it would be better not to tell Frances, I agreed.'

'Did he say *why* it would be better not to tell her?'

'He didn't have to, with Frances in such a fragile state.'

'How did he sound — did he sound shocked himself?'

'He sounded tired, empty. He'd been with the police for several hours,' she added quickly.

'*How* did he describe what had happened?'

'I don't understand what you mean . . . '

'Did he say that Dr Flint had been murdered, or did he say that there'd been an accident?'

'He said that she'd been killed and the police were treating it as suspicious.'

'Did he tell you it was he who'd found the body?'

'Yes, he did.'

'Didn't it occur to you then that he might be in trouble?'

'No, not at all.'

188

'Did he speak to Frances?'

'Yes, and he covered up remarkably well. She had no idea what had happened and was quite happy about spending the night here.'

Tom asked her about the next morning and she told him how Frances had come down tight-lipped and said she didn't want any breakfast, and how when she'd tried persuading her, Frances had suddenly 'flipped', sweeping the breakfast things on to the floor, screaming and then collapsing in tears.

'Has she ever shown any signs of doing anything like that before?'

'No. Never. It must have been the drug. I'd had my doubts when Fraser first told me, but not after that, Mr Jones.'

'You met Dr Flint, didn't you, Mrs Templeton?'

'Yes, and at first I thought how lucky Frances was to have someone like that to look after her . . . ' She broke down briefly, then recovered. 'And I thought Fraser was wrong, both about her and the drug, but not now, Mr Jones, not now.'

'D'you think he killed her?'

Her head came up sharply. 'Not for one moment. I've come to like and respect Fraser a great deal and I don't believe it for a moment. The police are making a terrible mistake.' She paused fractionally, said, 'I thought you were trying to help him, Mr Jones.'

'I'm trying to discover the truth.'

She said, 'If you do that, then you'll be helping him.'

15

Tom had just picked up the phone in his hotel room to bring Marcus up to date when he remembered Dr Weisman. He glanced at his watch — five thirty, which made it twelve thirty in New York. He found the number Fraser had given him and caught Weisman on his way to lunch.

'Gee, I'm sorry to hear that . . . ' was his obviously sincere reaction to the news about Fraser. He went on to confirm everything Fraser had said about Alkovin.

'People're beginning to notice these side-effects over here now. I guess it's only a matter of time before they take the stuff off the market.'

'Won't they just recommend using prophylactic antidepressants?'

'I think the problems with this drug go deeper than that.'

'In what way?'

Weisman hesitated. 'Let's just say its initial promise as a leukaemia treatment doesn't look so bright now,' he said at last.

Which wasn't good news for poor Frances, Tom thought as he broke the connection and phoned Marcus.

'I've fixed up interviews with Ian Saunders and Leo Farleigh for you tomorrow and the day after,' Marcus told him.

'Good. They didn't make any difficulties, then?'

'They made plenty. They were far too busy, they'd already spoken to the police and didn't see why they should speak to you. I had to get quite heavy with them in the end.'

Tom smiled. Marcus' usual method of 'getting heavy' was to inform his victims (in the most gentle of voices) that his next call would be to the top — in this case, either to the Trust general manager, or the managing director of Parc-Reed. He hadn't had to carry out the threat very often.

'So what times am I seeing them?'

'Saunders first thing tomorrow, at nine. By the way, he's also arranging for you to talk to Terry Stroud, the lab manager.'

'Good, I'd been wondering about him. What about Farleigh?'

'Well, he claimed he was unavailable for the rest of the week, but then he, too, discovered a hitherto unnoticed slot in his diary — for the following morning at his house.' He gave Tom the address.

★ ★ ★

192

Although Tom planned his interviews in advance to some extent, the tone and timing of his questions tended to follow his on-the-spot judgements of the interviewee's character and state of mind.

Ian Saunders now . . . what would get behind the impermeable smiling mask he presented?

'I believe the pressure for the trial with Alkovin came from yourself and Dr Flint?'

Ian smiled. 'That's correct, although I'm not sure I care for the word *pressure*.'

'Which of you was the first to hear about the drug?'

'Leo Farleigh put the idea to Connie at a conference, she persuaded me and we both went to John Somersby.'

'Who promptly squashed the idea?'

Again Ian smiled, although by now it was becoming a little strained.

'It *wasn't* promptly, it was after about two weeks — and I fail to see the need for such — er — emotive language.'

'Shall we say veto then? Why did Dr Somersby veto the idea?'

'He said he'd heard rumours of side-effects. He refused, however, to divulge the source of these rumours.'

'But you disagreed with him?'

'Connie and I both disagreed with him.'

'And then he was killed?'

The smile vanished. 'What are you trying to suggest, Mr Jones?'

'I'm not trying to suggest anything.' Yet . . . 'I'm merely stating facts.'

'It was at least six months afterwards that he was killed.'

'And then you took over as acting director?'

Ian compressed his lips before replying. 'Yes.'

'So it would have been your decision to overturn Dr Somersby's veto and go ahead with the trial?'

'No, it was a joint decision. Although I was nominally acting director, Connie and I agreed to run the department between us.'

'Were you surprised when she got the director's job?'

Ian took a breath before replying. 'Not entirely, no. We had similar qualifications and experience and there had been a lot of talk about there not being enough women in senior posts, so no, I wasn't really surprised.'

'So you're saying she owed her position to political correctness?'

'If you're trying to suggest there was any animosity between us, Mr Jones, you'd be quite wrong. We ran the department together both before and after she became director.'

'A sort of joint leadership?'

'That's right.'

'So it would be fair to say that you had joint responsibility for the decisions taken thereafter?'

Ian's mouth tightened briefly as he realised how he'd been manoeuvred into this admission. He covered it by saying, 'I'm beginning to feel like a hostile witness at a trial — a legal one, that is. Yes, Connie did usually consult me before taking any decisions, even though she was director.'

Tom was sure by now that Ian's strategy was to try and shuffle any blame on to Connie. He said, 'About nine months into the trial, Dr Callan tried to draw your attention to the side-effects of the drug he'd noticed?'

'He tried to draw *Connie's* attention — I really must make it clear that, in the main, his dispute was with Connie.'

Tom said incredulously, 'Are you trying to tell me you didn't agree with her?'

'No, I'm not telling you that. I'm telling you that there were emotive reasons for their quarrel as well as medical ones.'

'You'll have to explain.'

'Will I really?' It was Ian's turn to be incredulous. 'I can't believe that you don't know about the fling they had.'

'Yes, I do know as it happens, from the

police, who got it from you. The question is, how did *you* know?'

'Connie let it slip one evening in her cups.' He paused, then said, 'She was drinking a lot in the last year of her life.'

'Why was that, d'you think?'

'I believe the strain of being in charge was more than she'd anticipated.'

'Even though it was a joint leadership?'

'Even so.'

'Let's get back to Alkovin and Dr Callan. He tried to bring to your, and Dr Flint's, attention the side-effects he'd noticed, didn't he?'

'One of his patients had tried to kill himself and he took it more personally than perhaps he should. He did tend to become emotionally involved with patients.'

'But that wasn't the only evidence, was it?'

'We looked at that evidence very carefully, Mr Jones. It was badly put together, much of it hearsay and some, we felt, frankly exaggerated.'

'D'you still think that?'

Ian said carefully, 'I think that Connie's decision to ignore it, *based on what we knew at the time*, was the right one.'

Tom declined the offered bait. 'But then, a few months later, after a successful suicide, Dr Callan assembled more data, including some from Birmingham, and still you wouldn't listen. In fact, you sent him away on sabbatical to shut him up.'

Ian was smiling again. 'You seem to be suggesting that I was personally responsible for that, Mr Jones.'

He told Tom what had happened and his account didn't differ significantly from Fraser's. 'The fact is, I was beginning to have doubts about Alkovin myself by then — '

Here it comes.

' — but Connie was furious with Fraser for going behind her back, which made her react perhaps more strongly than she should.'

'So you're trying to tell me *now* that you had worries about Alkovin *then?*'

'Yes, I am,' Ian said, ignoring the scorn in Tom's voice. 'As I was telling you, Fraser went first to Robert Swann, our junior consultant, and he came to me. We agreed that there were grounds for disquiet, but felt we had no choice but to tell Connie. Predictably, perhaps, she erupted. Speak to Robert, he'll confirm what I say.'

I bet he will, thought Tom. Which way to go . . . ? Saunders obviously thought he'd successfully offloaded the responsibility. He said, 'What I'm having difficulty with, Dr Saunders, is that if you were worried *then,* why didn't you do something *then?*'

'With Connie's frame of mind at that time, it was frankly impossible. Now, we're recommending prophylactic antidepressants for all our patients on Alkovin.'

'Since when was this?'

'Since Frances Templeton's unhappy experience.'

'D'you think Dr Callan killed Dr Flint?'

If Ian felt any surprise at the timing of this question, he didn't show it.

'It grieves me to say so, but I can see no other explanation. We know that Fraser was in a highly volatile state because of Frances' illness and depression, and that he held Connie personally responsible for that depression — to the extent of threatening her. Then she had him suspended for assaulting her — I was there at the time — '

'You actually saw it?'

'I heard Connie scream and went to investigate . . . ' He described what he'd seen, and again, his account didn't differ in its facts from Fraser's, although he managed to imply a greater violence on his part. 'So I'm afraid I'm forced to the conclusion that he did kill her.'

'Did you know that the value of Parc-Reed shares has doubled in the last year?'

Ian went still. 'I . . . believe I'd heard

something to that effect. What's the relevance?'

'Do you own, or have you owned any Parc-Reed shares?'

'This is becoming positively McCarthyite.'

Tom made no reply to this, and after a pause Ian went on, 'I'm sure a glance at the public register will have already given you the answer to that question.'

'There are ways of buying shares other than through the public register.'

'I'll take your word for that,' Ian said in a still voice. 'Am I to know the point of these questions?'

Tom said carefully, 'Dr Callan, when he came to see us, was at a loss for an explanation of your persistent refusal to address his concerns over Alkovin.'

'I thought I'd already made that clear to you, Mr Jones. Had it been me, I would have given his concerns more attention. But it wasn't me, it was Dr Flint, with whom Dr Callan had an emotionally destructive relationship.'

'And yet it was Dr Flint who phoned Dr Callan, told him that she'd changed her mind and asked him to come to her house to discuss it.'

'I believe I'm right in saying that we have only Dr Callan's word for that.'

'She told him she was worried about 'the others'. D'you have any idea who these 'others' might be?'

Ian regarded Tom with frank loathing for a moment before replying: 'Dr Callan has been charged with murder and I question the need to take seriously anything he may have said. I'm a busy man, Mr Jones.' He stood up. 'Was there anything else before I take you along to Mr Stroud?'

'Yes,' said Tom, not moving. 'Where were you on Saturday morning, between say ten and twelve?'

'As I've already told the police, at home with my wife.'

There was no point in going any further, so Tom smiled and said, 'Thank you, Dr Saunders. I'll see Mr Stroud now, if I may.'

'I'll take you there.'

16

In Fraser's dream, Frances was in a whirlpool and he was reaching down, trying to take her outstretched hand, when a Welsh sergeant major shouted at him and pulled him back and he could only watch as she —

'Wakey wakey rise and shine my lovely boys.'

He opened his eyes as a fist banged against the door and there was a click as it was unlocked.

'Feckin' bastard,' he shouted before he could stop himself and heard Petru chuckle.

The door slid open and a bulky prison officer stepped in. 'Fucking bastard, is it? So who's the comedian in here, then?'

'I'm sorry,' Fraser said. 'I was dreaming.'

'Well, I don't like dreams like that.' He pointed his baton, gave him a playful jab on the nose with it. 'OK?'

'OK,' said Fraser. 'Sorry.'

The officer left and Fraser looked at his watch. It was seven o'clock and he felt terrible.

They got up and went along to the shower

room. Ilie 'slopped out', took the chemical bog and emptied its contents into a sluice. Then they dressed and went to breakfast. Some sense of irony in Fraser's nature made him choose porridge.

At the table, Ilie said, 'Fraser, you come class?'

'What class?'

'Eenglish.'

Might as well. 'All right.'

The class was 'English as a foreign language', which was of no use whatsoever to Fraser, although, as the teacher explained to him, his presence might be a great deal of use to the others there.

How the hell do you teach English to a bunch of assorted foreigners (besides the four Romanians, there were a Dutchman, a Finn and two Spaniards) while having no knowledge of their various languages?

The teacher, an attractive woman in her forties, started with a picture, a treasure chest. She spelt the word *chest*, and from there went to *church*, *chopper* and so on. Fraser soon picked it up and found that he could really help, and for the first time since his arrival, actually forgot where he was for a moment.

After the English class came the exercise period and Fraser, assuming he'd be in the same group as the Romanians, tagged along with them.

'Class — good?' Ilie asked as they went up a wide flight of stairs, watched by an officer on the next landing.

Fraser nodded. 'Yes.'

'You come again?'

'All right.'

'Thank you.' Ilie touched his shoulder, aware that the benefit was all one way.

As they went through the door at the top, daylight exploded around Fraser and he stopped dead, blinded and disorientated. *I've been here less than twenty-four hours. Am I becoming institutionalised already?*

The two other Romanians had started talking to his cell mates and he wandered over to the rail by himself, looking round as his eyes became accustomed to the brightness.

The upper deck forming the exercise yard was about fifty by a hundred feet and a fence beyond the rail ran all the way round the perimeter. This was constructed of what seemed to be a continuous sheet of metal with oval holes cut into it so that it consisted more of hole than metal. The effect was like a chain link fence; the difference being that if you were foolish enough to try and climb it, your fingers would be cut to pieces on the sharp metal edges. It extended up for about ten feet, where it inclined inwards and was coiled about with razor wire.

He looked round the yard. Prisoners wandered in groups, chatting, smoking, chewing gum. Two or three officers guarded them. They talked to the prisoners amicably enough when addressed, but watchfully, always watchful.

He peered through the fence and after a while it ceased to obstruct his vision. The sea twinkled and flashed with white horses and sunlight. Gulls bobbed in the swell and the air was heavy with salt. In the distance lay the multi-coloured tinsel of a town — Weymouth, he assumed. To the right, a soft, indistinct coastline and to the left, the causeway to the island.

Boats were scattered around: big, small, some moored to buoys, others to the wharf. Some were smart, some scruffy — as he watched, a herring gull that was perched on one of the latter defecated as it rose screaming into the air, leaving a new smear down the cabin window.

He filled his lungs with the salty, springy air and walked slowly round the perimeter. There were benches and a few tables, bare torsos, several languages and always the fence. Another seagull wheeled and wailed overhead and the sound made him stop and clench his eyes shut in misery . . .

After a moment, he opened them again and resumed walking. No one seemed to have noticed him. He still felt disorientated, utterly detached from what was going on around him.

From nowhere, the words *Physician heal thyself* flashed into his mind and he thought, *Institutionalised be buggered, I'm still in shock.* The realisation didn't heal him, but the understanding helped.

The exercise period ended and Ilie came to find him.

'You come — machine shop?'

Fraser smiled and shook his head. 'I'll see you back in the cell, Ilie.'

He wanted time to explore his new-found understanding.

★   ★   ★

Ian silently led Tom to Terry's room, knocked on the door and opened it — a tangible sign of rank, Tom reflected; you might knock at an underling's door, but you don't wait for an invitation before going in.

'Oh, hello, Dr Saunders.' The man inside got to his feet.

205

'Terry, this is Mr Jones from the Department of Health. He wants to interrogate you. I'll leave you to it.' He withdrew, obviously still smarting from his own interrogation.

'Er — come in, Mr Jones.' Tom took the proffered hand, which was rock hard. 'Have a seat ... Interrogate, I think Dr Saunders said?'

'Just his sense of fun, I expect,' Tom said as he sat down.

'I see. Well, how can I help you?'

Tom began explaining about Fraser's allegation, but Terry interrupted him: 'I'm afraid I can't help you there. Drug treatment is outside my area of competence.'

This didn't altogether surprise Tom, bearing in mind Fraser's description and his own observations — the rigidity of body and handshake, the I-know-my-place speech and accent.

'I appreciate that,' he said, 'but you can probably help more than you think. For instance, I believe you overheard Dr Callan apparently threatening Dr Flint?'

'Well, yes, I did, and there was no apparently about it.'

'Would you like to tell me what happened?'

Of course he would ... 'Well, it was Saturday — I always come in of a Saturday to make sure everything's all right ... '

That figures.

'I saw Dr Callan coming in and said hello, since I hadn't seen him for three months. He was rather brusque and I remember thinking at the time he must have heard about Frances — she's his fiancée.'

'I know about Frances,' said Tom.

'Well, he was looking pale and angry and I saw him go into Dr Flint's room. I needed to see her myself as it happened, nothing really urgent, but instinct made me go down after a few minutes and I heard the whole thing.'

He paused — for effect, Tom assumed. 'What did you hear?'

'They were arguing — he called her something . . . blinkered bitch, I think it was. Anyway, she told him to go, very calm like, and he said he'd hold her personally responsible if anything happened to Frances. Then she said, and I remember this exactly, 'Are you threatening me, Fraser?' And he said, 'Yes, I am threatening you . . . ' '

'Are you sure those are the exact words?'

'Yes, I am sure.' Terry's mild eyes gazed back at him.

'All right, go on.'

'Well, she laughed at him, said, 'What can you do to me?' Then she said, 'You only know about violence, don't you? Are you going to kill me?' And then — '

'How exactly did she say that?' Tom interrupted. 'Was she still laughing at him?'

'Oh yes, she didn't take him seriously, see, more's the pity. Anyway, he said, 'If anything happens to Frances, I will kill you.' Then he realised I was there an' looked round and I'm telling you, one look at his face made *me* take him seriously.'

This would be powerful stuff in a courtroom, Tom realised.

'You don't like Dr Callan much, do you?'

Again, the honest serving man's look. 'No, Mr Jones, I can't say that I do.'

'Why is that?'

Terry thought for a moment, then said, 'Dr Flint was a lady. Dr Callan is a jumped-up nobody.'

When he was sure Terry wasn't going to add anything, Tom said, 'You and he had crossed swords before, hadn't you?'

'That depends on what you mean by crossed swords.'

'Didn't you have a disagreement with him about issuing lab results?'

'Yes, I did. He'd been a lab worker himself once and thought that entitled him to tell me how to do my job.'

'You can't have enjoyed that very much,' Tom said.

'I didn't. I don't tell the doctors how to

treat patients and I don't expect them to tell me how to manage my staff.'

'Fair enough, I'd have thought. What happened exactly?'

'Well, I went to point out to Steve Lovell that he'd issued an unauthorised result — there's no harm in the lad, he just needed putting right — and Dr Callan overruled me.'

'What, there and then?'

'Yes. I pointed out to him that it was against regulations and he just pooh-poohed me. None of the other doctors ever had.'

'I see what you mean,' said Tom. *Get off the subject* . . . 'You said just now that Dr Flint was a lady — would you say the same of Dr Saunders?'

'Yes. Although in his case,' he added with a chuckle, 'I'd say gent.'

Tom chuckled too. 'Sure. How about Dr Somersby?'

' . . . Oh yes, he was a gent too.' A fraction's hesitation.

'Were you aware that Dr Callan had recommended you be offered early retirement?'

Terry's eyes flashed. 'That doesn't surprise me,' he said evenly.

'Early retirement doesn't appeal to you?'

'I believe I still have some service left in me.'

'Of course,' said Tom. 'Well, I think that's all I need from you for now.' He stood up. 'Thanks very much.'

'You're very welcome.'

They shook hands again and Tom left.

Is he a fruitcase or what . . . ? He'd egged Terry on, then cut the interview short, hopefully before he could get any inkling of his interest.

But Terry was also, he realised as he climbed into his car, potential dynamite in court — for either side, depending on how he was handled.

He had a pub lunch, then drove up to the downs that overlooked the city and lit a cheroot. It was tempting to go and see Agnes and tell her about Terry now, but on reflection he decided to wait until he'd seen Leo the next day. He went back to the hotel and wrote up the two interviews.

★ ★ ★

Leo lived in a large detached house in a close on the edge of the city; there was no doubt, Tom thought as he drew up beside it the next morning, that repping, Leo-style, had doctoring beat for money.

The man himself came to the door and showed Tom into a living-room. One glance told Tom that Leo lived alone, and had done for some time — it was clean and tidy enough, but completely devoid of the touches a woman would have given it.

'Coffee?'

'Please.'

'Milk and sugar?'

'Milk but no sugar, thanks.'

The sofa that Tom sank into was of real leather. There was a large TV and a small bookcase with no fiction. Large reproductions of Picasso and other relatively modern artists graced the walls. Nothing wrong with that, Tom reflected, but it was as though Leo had marched into a shop and said, 'I'll take that one, that one and that one . . .'

Leo came back into the room with a tray. 'There you go.' He wore designer jeans, a cashmere sweater and loafers — very casual, and very expensive. He took a mug and sat down himself. 'Fire away.'

The words somehow suggested to Tom that Leo considered himself fireproof, so he decided to mix his metaphors and shoot from the hip.

'Dr Callan told us when he came to see us that he thought there was corruption involved in the taking on and trial of Alkovin.'

'Well, he would say something like that, wouldn't he?' Not fazed in the least.

'How d'you mean?' Tom asked.

'I mean that he isn't really in a position to pontificate on anything at the moment, is he? Not when he's banged up in prison charged with murder.'

And in no small part due to you, Tom thought. 'Nevertheless, such allegations have to be investigated.'

Leo leaned forward. 'From the out, Fraser was obsessed with Alkovin's *alleged* side-effects — so some idea of conspiracy or corruption would be the only explanation that could satisfy him.'

His accent, Tom thought, was a mixture of local and mid-Atlantic. 'Are you saying he's wrong about the side-effects?'

'Yes, I am.'

'It does seem to me that there's some acceptance of them now. Even Dr Saunders told me yesterday that there's a case for treating patients on Alkovin with prophylactic antidepressants.'

Leo shrugged. 'Maybe there's occasional transient depression, although it's far from proven that Alkovin is the cause. The fact remains that it's an invaluable drug for treating lymphoblastic leukaemia.'

'I wouldn't have described what Frances Templeton went through as transient.'

'She's an exception.'

'The one that proves the rule, perhaps?'

Leo leaned back. 'Those are your words.'

'Where was Alkovin developed?'

'In the States, by our parent company.'

He explained how after successful Phase One and Two trials there, the company wanted to introduce it to the UK.

Phase One and Two trials? Tom queried.

Phase One, Leo told him, was to use the drug on terminal patients who had nothing to lose and perhaps something to gain, while Phase Two was a direct comparison of the drug on non-terminal patients with other, established drugs. 'If there were any serious side-effects, we'd have learned about them at that stage,' he said.

'Wouldn't that depend on how long the trials lasted? I understand these side-effects don't appear until after the second or third round of treatment.'

'The trials are designed to take that into account.'

'And yet,' Tom persisted, 'Dr Somersby refused to take on the drug over here because of what an American colleague had told him about it.'

'That was hearsay, the source of which Dr Somersby refused to divulge. We made enquiries, but picked up nothing ourselves.'

'We?'

'Myself and my own American colleagues.'

'But after Dr Somersby had been murdered, and Alkovin taken on, Dr Callan repeatedly produced evidence to the contrary — didn't this make you wonder at all?'

'Sure it did. We looked at Dr Callan's evidence very carefully on each occasion and concluded that it didn't stand up.'

'We?'

'Myself, Dr Flint and Dr Saunders.'

'I didn't realise you were qualified to make medical judgements, Mr Farleigh,' Tom sniped.

'Perhaps not on my own, Mr Jones, no. Certainly no more than you are to question me about it now.'

'*Touché*,' Tom said, understanding why Leo was such a successful company rep. 'It seems ironic though, doesn't it, that after all Dr Callan's efforts, his fiancée should be the one to prove him right?'

'Frances' unfortunate experience is in no way proof of anything. What it *does* explain is Fraser's emotional judgements concerning Alkovin, not to mention the subsequent tragedy.'

Time for a switch. 'Are you aware of how much Parc-Reed shares have risen over the last year?'

'Sure. We're all very pleased about it.' No

hesitation, not bothered in the least.

'How many do *you* own?'

'Two thousand. A company bonus. A lot of us got them.'

'Someone who owned a large block would make a lot of money.'

'I imagine they would.'

'How much of that rise is due to the apparent success of Alkovin?'

Leo spread his hands and shrugged. 'You tell me. I expect it has some bearing.'

'So it would be to the advantage of someone owning a lot of shares if any — er — negative information concerning Alkovin could be suppressed?'

Leo leaned back in his chair with an expression of frank dislike. 'Just what are you getting at, Mr Jones?'

'I'd have thought that was obvious. Dr Callan says that Alkovin is dangerous and I've just outlined a very clear motive for suppressing such information.'

'As I told you just now, I own two thousand Parc-Reed shares given me as a bonus by the company. You can check that on the public register, if you haven't already. I don't know how many other people own and I don't think there's any point in further discussion of this topic.'

He got to his feet, but Tom said

deliberately, 'I haven't finished yet.'

They stared at each other a moment before Leo resumed his seat. Tom said, 'Dr Callan told me that Dr Flint had come round to his way of thinking, that's why she phoned and asked him to come to her house that Saturday.'

'And I repeat,' said Leo, 'he would say something like that, wouldn't he?'

'Why were you there, Mr Farleigh?'

'I'd just been faxed some new data on Alkovin from the States that I thought she'd want to see.'

'On a *Saturday?*'

'Sure. I'm married to my job, Mr Jones. So was she.'

'But Dr Callan says you told him that Dr Flint had phoned you.'

'No, he asked me whether she had phoned me and I said yes. I'd just found Dr Callan with her dead body — I'd have agreed with anything he said at that moment. My one idea was to get the police as quickly as possible.'

'D'you still have this data you were going to show her?'

'Sure I do, it's somewhere at the office. D'you want me to look it out for you?'

'If you would, please.'

'Was there anything else before you go?'

There wasn't a lot. Tom had just about

exhausted his locker and Leo knew it. 'Yes. You said in your statement to the police that Dr Callan was still holding the stick when you found him with Dr Flint's body?'

'That's right.'

'Would you show me?'

Leo gave a short laugh. 'What d'you mean, show you?'

Tom looked round the room, got up and fetched an umbrella. 'This'll do for the stick.' He handed it to the bemused Leo. 'And this'll do for Dr Flint.' He placed a cushion on the floor. 'Now, show me what Dr Callan was doing when you found him.'

With a look at Tom, Leo knelt beside the cushion, touched it with his left hand while holding the umbrella in his right. 'He was touching her head, like this, and holding the stick like this . . . ' He somehow managed to imbue the pose with infinite malice.

'OK, thanks,' said Tom. 'That'll be all for now — oh, that material you're going to send me — will you be in your office this afternoon? I'll come and collect it.'

'I hadn't intended to be.'

'Tomorrow morning, then? I really would like to see it.'

'All right,' Leo said resignedly, 'tomorrow morning. D'you know how to find us?' He gave him instructions.

17

Tom phoned Agnes from his car and she told him she could see him in half an hour, so he smoked a contemplative cheroot while he thought about Leo and the things he'd said. Would a guilty person have reacted with such in-your-face defiance? he wondered. Or maybe he really did consider himself fireproof . . .

He made some notes in his book, then drove down to the city centre and looked for somewhere to park.

'I'm sure they're both liars,' he told Agnes in her office, 'but I don't know how much that helps you.'

'What are they lying about, exactly?' She was wearing a blue dress that set off the colour of her limpid eyes.

'Well, Saunders firstly tried to heap all the blame for Alkovin on to Dr Flint, then waxed most indignant when I brought up the subject of shares.'

'Protesting too much?'

'Far too much. Farleigh more or less looked me in the eye and dared me to prove it.' He gave her the gist of the two interviews.

'But you think all three of them had shares and were trying to up the price?'

'Farleigh, certainly. The other two? Well, maybe they started out genuinely believing in the drug and didn't see any harm in a little part-time insider dealing . . . but there's no doubt that when Callan tried to warn them about the side-effects, they not only wilfully ignored him, but actively tried to suppress him . . . So yes, I do.'

'D'you think either of them killed Somersby?'

'The police didn't think so . . . and it would imply a level of premeditation and ruthlessness I wouldn't have credited them with.'

'Not even Farleigh?'

'Well, possibly Farleigh . . . '

Agnes leaned forward slightly. 'Could either Farleigh or Saunders have killed Dr Flint?'

'Again, the police don't think so.'

'But what do *you* think, Mr Jones?'

After a pause, Tom sighed. 'I don't know.'

'All right . . . but it would still help Fraser if we could show they were corrupt, wouldn't it?'

Tom took a breath, released it. 'It might. But then again, supposing we were able to prove it, the prosecution could argue that the fact Dr Flint used Alkovin on Callan's fiancée *knowing* its dangers makes an even stronger motive for him killing her.'

'But her phone call — she'd changed her mind about it.'

'We still only have his word for that.'

'But if you're right about Saunders and Farleigh, it gives *them* a motive for killing her as well, doesn't it?'

'Only if they knew she changed her mind — assuming she did change it. And how *could* they know? Callan himself said she told him she was worried *in case* they found out.'

'No he didn't,' Agnes said. She rummaged among the papers on her desk for a moment. 'He said that she told him to come as soon as he could, because 'I'm worried about the others.' ' She looked up. 'I think the best defence is that they were all three corrupt, and that Farleigh and Saunders have just as strong motives for killing her as Fraser.'

'You could be right,' agreed Tom, 'but how the hell we go about proving it, I've no idea.'

'What about the public register of shares?'

'We've already looked,' he said, and told her what he'd discovered about nominee accounts.

'But couldn't we get a court order to make the broker tell us the truth?'

'Certainly we could, so long as we first

found which broker they'd used. There are thousands of them and they're bound to have picked one miles away — Liverpool, or somewhere. Besides,' he continued, 'I don't mind betting they've already taken the money and run.'

'Sold the shares, you mean? Mightn't that be the way of nailing them?'

'How d'you mean?'

'There must be records of share sales. Couldn't we look up recent large sales and trace them back to the brokers?'

'We could try, but millions, *billions*, of shares change hands every day. And their blocks wouldn't be that large compared with the big insurance companies and pension funds.' He paused. 'I'll look into it when I get back.'

She said tentatively, 'There is one other possibility . . . '

He waited.

'I had a phone call from the police this morning. Sebi Flint, that's Dr Flint's son, is her executor and he's asked them whether he can start going through some of her effects. Garrett rang to ask whether I had any objections.'

'And had you?'

'I said no at the time, but it's occurred to me since that she might have had an address book or something, some record of the name of her broker.'

Tom's mind raced as he mentally kicked himself — he'd been in the house, at her desk, only two days before . . .

'Did the police give any indication of when Master Flint would be likely to start?' he asked.

'No. Obviously, they'd have had to get back to him first — '

'Which they've probably already done by now.'

'But would he necessarily want to start immediately?'

'He might. What are you suggesting, that we tell Garrett?'

Agnes made a noise somewhere between a grunt and a snort. 'A minute's exposure to *him* and Sebi'd certainly destroy any evidence. *You*, on the other hand . . . '

'Yes?' said Tom when he realised she wasn't going to go on.

'Well, you're more subtle, more . . . ' She waved her hand in the air.

'Yes?'

'All right, you're more devious and less scrupulous, more likely to find something.'

Tom decided he rather liked Agnes Croft. He smiled and said, 'I may or may not be worthy of your flattery . . . D'you happen to know where Sebi's staying at the moment?'

'Yes — with his father.'

'D'you know his number?' A nod. 'Ring him now, tell him you need to talk to him now, here in your office . . . Go on.'

She found the number, dialled, waited. 'No answer.'

'Keep trying, and get him in here if you can.' He gave her his car phone number and stood up. 'Keep me in touch.'

'Where are you going?'

'To his mother's.'

★ ★ ★

He parked in the road and walked up the tree-lined drive — Bugger! There was a white Nissan outside the house, Sebi's, he assumed. Nothing to lose, try to bluff him . . .

He rang the bell and a fresh-faced youth in his late teens with blue eyes and fair hair opened the door. Tom apologised for intruding, explained who he was and showed him his identification.

'You can ring the Department of Health and check if you like,' he said.

'I think I will,' said Sebi, and shut the door.

He opened it again a few minutes later and said without a great deal of enthusiasm,

223

'You'd better come in.' He led him through the tiled outer hall (the marks had been removed) to an inner hall and then into a living-room. It was elegantly furnished with plenty of books and pictures, although it already held the slight mustiness of disuse.

'Have a seat.' Sebi indicated an armchair.

Now for the tricky bit, thought Tom, and told him about Fraser's visit to himself and Marcus just before his mother's death.

Sebi stiffened. 'Are you telling me you're trying to help the man who murdered my mother?'

'No, I'm not telling you that, Mr Flint. The allegation was made and we have to look into it whether we like it or not. But we do so from a completely neutral standpoint.'

'Well, he was lying,' Sebi said hotly. 'Lying to try and save his skin.'

'For what it's worth,' said Tom, lying himself now, 'I think you're probably right — especially when you consider what happened afterwards.' He didn't always like his job.

Sebi said, 'My mother was absolutely dedicated to her profession, she'd *never* have got mixed up in tacky share dealing.'

'I'm sure that's true,' said Tom, 'but as I said, once an allegation's made, we're bound to investigate it.'

'I suppose so,' Sebi said a little more reasonably.

Tom said carefully, 'Let me be devil's advocate for a moment. You said your mother wouldn't have got mixed up in share dealing, but what about after she divorced? She'd have been short of money then.'

'No, she became even more dedicated after that. I think she wanted to prove that she was as good a professional as my father . . . She wanted Alkovin to succeed, but she'd never knowingly have promoted a dangerous drug. It simply wasn't in her.' He paused. 'So I don't see how I can help you, Mr Jones.'

'I understand you've been checking over some of your mother's effects?'

'Yes.' He gave a tight humourless smile. 'She made me executor and our solicitor thought it might be an idea.'

'Did she have an address book?'

'Yes.' He was on his guard again. 'Why d'you ask?'

'Would you mind if I had a look at it?'

'Yes, I think I would rather. Can you explain why?'

The most delicate moment . . .

'I want to check for the names of any stockbrokers.'

It took him a second to work it out. 'Of all the bloody nerve!' He stood up. 'I thought you said you were neutral — you're assuming her guilt — '

'Will you listen a moment — *please*. I believe you're studying medicine at university yourself, aren't you?'

A nod.

'Then you'll be aware that very often, the best way to test a hypothesis is to try to show the opposite. Then, when you fail, you have powerful evidence that your hypothesis is the truth.'

He watched Sebi work it out, hoping he wouldn't spot the obvious flaws.

'All right, but I don't believe it.'

He quickly left the room and came back a few moments later with a slim book. Tom opened it and flicked the pages — it was well filled.

'Have the police seen this?'

'Yes.'

'Could I keep it for a day or two?'

'No, I don't like the idea of that.'

A push too far . . . 'Fair enough. I'll need a little time to look at it here, then.'

He took Sebi's silence for acquiescence and turned his attention to the book. The obvious thing to do was note down any names that sounded like firms, although his gut feeling was that it was more likely to be under a name like Paul or Stephanie . . . or maybe he should look at the latest entries for each letter . . .

He took out his notebook and had reached E when Sebi got up and looked out of the window.

'It's Dad, excuse me . . . ' He left the room again.

Tom thought quickly. Flint senior would almost certainly take a dim view of his presence. Should he take the book and run for it? No . . . He turned to the very end, where he himself sometimes noted numbers that didn't fit anywhere else . . . Sure enough, there were three, headed F, P and one on its own. He scribbled them down and had just put his notebook away when a bullfrog of a man strode into the room.

'You can hand that over right now,' he said, standing over Tom with outstretched paw.

'OK,' said Tom equably and held it up. It was snatched away.

'Now, who the hell are you?'

Tom stood up and produced his ID, then watched as the man studied it. He was over six feet, smartly dressed and with a handsome face that was just beginning to run to dissipation. He looked about fifty.

He flicked the card back to Tom. 'My son said you had a notebook — I'll trouble you for that as well.' He held out his hand.

Tom said, 'I am speaking to Dr Flint, I assume?'

'*Mister* Flint — I'm a surgeon.'

'Well, Mr Flint, the address book is yours, or at least, your son's — but the notebook is mine.'

'Not the information you wrote in it.'

Tom smiled and shook his head. 'Your son, who is his mother's executor, allowed me to copy it, and the notebook and its contents are mine.'

Flint dropped his hand. 'All right . . . if that's your attitude, you can get out.' He gestured towards the door.

As Tom passed him, Flint grabbed the fingers of his right hand and, bending them apart, forced his arm up behind his back. 'Get it, Sebi, quick!'

Tom struggled, but his fingers were twisted further apart and his arm yanked up. 'Keep still . . . Come on, Sebi . . . '

As Sebi reluctantly came forward, Tom glanced down, took aim and slammed his heel on to Flint's instep as hard as he could — the instep being the second most sensitive body part of the human male.

Flint gave a gratifying howl and collapsed on to the floor, nursing it.

'What have you done?' said Sebi.

'Stepped on his toe,' said Tom. 'Excuse me.'

Sebi went over to his father as Tom left the room. 'That's assault,' he shouted after him. 'I'll have the police on to you for this.'

Next to Sebi's Nissan was a very smart black Mercedes sports car, the sort that quietly makes a Porsche look like a toy. Being a surgeon evidently paid even better than a rep on the make, Tom reflected.

His car phone was ringing as he got to the Cooper.

'Hello?'

'Tom, it's Agnes. I still haven't been able to contact him.'

'I think I'd worked that out,' Tom said and told her what had happened.

She sighed. 'You'd better get down here and we'll put a statement together . . . '

After they'd done it, they phoned Garrett, then took it along to him at the police station.

'Why didn't you tell us about the address book?' Garrett demanded after he'd read the statement.

'I assumed you'd already seen it.'

'Then why not *ask* us about it instead of barging in where you're not wanted? All right, I know, you were only doing your job . . . Were you intending to stay in Avon much longer, Mr Jones?'

'I'd have been on my way home by now if it wasn't for this.'

'Well, you can do me a favour by doing that and staying there, sir. We'll sort out Mr Flint.'

In the event, they went back to Agnes' office and tried the phone numbers Tom had found. There was a chiropractor, a health farm, a personal friend, and, most surprisingly, a dating agency. But there was no stockbroker.

★ ★ ★

Fraser continued going to the English classes with the Romanians, but one look, or listen rather, to the machine shop was enough for him and he went to the library instead. After flicking through a few thrillers, he decided on impulse to read *Don Quixote* — Cervantes had written it in prison, so the least he could do was read it.

Mary came to see him.

'How is she, Mary?'

'She's doing well. Once she's through with this round of treatment, she'll come and see you herself.'

Agnes came and told him about her adventures with Tom. He smiled when he heard about Charlie Flint's foot.

'At least he seems to be taking it seriously,' he said.

He came to value the exercise periods above all. It could so easily have driven him mad, he thought, the sights and sounds of freedom: the sea, the gulls, the comings and goings of the boats; instead, they became the things that kept him sane, saved him from becoming institutionalised.

There was a black fishing-boat that puttered back every afternoon from somewhere or other, a gin palace that had plenty of visitors but never seemed to go anywhere (although the owners couldn't be that loaded, he thought, or they'd have found a more prestigious location) and a scruffy little cruiser moored to the wharf on the seaward side of the ship that a man came to work on every morning. He obviously kept his equipment on board, because he arrived in fairly tidy jeans and T-shirt, vanished below and then reappeared in a boiler suit.

★   ★   ★

One evening about a week after he'd arrived, Fraser was waiting in the queue for the phone. It was fifteen minutes before lock-up and he was twitching with impatience, moving his weight from one foot to the other. With five minutes to go, the man ahead of him put the phone down and turned away. Fraser was moving forward when, from nowhere, someone stepped in front of him and picked it up.

'Hey!' said Fraser. 'Excuse me . . . '

The man turned and looked at him. 'Gotta n'urgent call — aw righ'?' He was about an inch shorter than Fraser with a round face, cropped hair and small pale blue eyes. He turned back to the phone.

'No, it's not all right,' Fraser said as someone behind him murmured:

'Leave it, mate, jus' leave it . . . '

The man turned again and fixed Fraser with his eyes. 'You dunno 'oo I am, do ya?'

'No, and I don't care,' Fraser said. 'You're — '

He didn't get any further because the man's forehead crunched into his nose and then his fist sank into his belly. He gagged and fell to his knees.

'What's this then?' Humber, one of the senior officers, had appeared. 'What you playing at, Sutton?'

Sutton said, 'Jockstrap 'ere tried to push in front of me an' got nasty when I wouldn't let 'im.'

'He's lying,' Fraser croaked from the floor.

The officer turned to the others. 'What happened?'

There was a pause. Sutton stared at the man behind Fraser who said reluctantly, 'It was like Sutton said.' The two others murmured agreement.

'All right, let's be 'aving you . . . ' Humber and another who'd joined him hauled Fraser to his feet and led him away to the first aid station.

'So what really happened?' he asked as he cleaned up Fraser's nose.

'He pushed in front of me and did this when I objected.' His nose felt twice its normal size.

'Thought it'd be somethin' like that.'

'Then why didn't you — '

'Because it's your word against Sutton and three others. No one argues with Mickey Sutton.'

'But that's intimidation . . . Who's running this place, you or him?'

'Listen, Callan — one day Sutton's goin' to slip up an' when he does, we'll hit him like a hundred tons of shit. But until then, you keep away from him. OK?'

'But — '

'You're not listening, Callan . . . I said, keep — away — from — him. Right?'

'All right.'

'He'll get his someday, I promise you that, but don't you have any part of it.'

Back in his cell, he told the others, who simply repeated what Humber had said.

'Him bad guy,' Ilie said. 'Don't mess.'

Petru had a bad summer cold and was even more taciturn than usual. He'd never been as friendly as Ilie, and Fraser didn't know whether it was because Petru resented him or whether he was just naturally that way.

He rolled another cigarette and lit it and broke into a fit of coughing, interspersed with Romanian swearing. He didn't put the fag out, though. Ilie caught Fraser's look and shrugged.

After lights out, Fraser couldn't sleep, partly because of the pain in his nose and belly and partly because Petru was making even more noise than usual — a mixture of snores, coughs and groans. As Fraser listened, the groaning got worse. Ilie said something in Romanian that probably meant Shut up, but Petru seemed beyond hearing.

Fraser sat up suddenly, listened a few more moments, then threw back the bedclothes and gingerly climbed down the ladder. Ilie opened his eyes and grumbled. Petru suddenly gave a deeper groan and tried to turn as he vomited. It spilled over the bed and floor.

'Ah fuckit,' said Ilie, reverting to English.

'He's ill,' Fraser said. 'I mean, really ill . . . '

Ignoring the vomit, he felt Petru's forehead, which was burning hot. He put his hand under the back of his head and tried to bend it forward, but Petru's neck remained absolutely rigid. He pulled back the bedclothes, felt under Petru's knee and eased his leg up, then tried pushing it down again . . . it wouldn't move. He examined his chest and belly, but couldn't see anything, so he rolled him over — Ah! About a dozen purple spots covering both cheeks.

'Meningococcal meningitis,' he said, as much to himself as Ilie. He went to the door and pounded on it with his fists. 'Hey, boss,' he shouted. 'Guv, come here, quick!'

Footsteps and a voice: 'All right, all right . . . you'd better have a fucking good reason for this, Callan.'

'It's Petru . . . ' Fraser couldn't remember his surname. 'He's ill, he's got meningitis.'

'How the fuck would you know . . . oh yeah, you're a doctor, aren't you?'

Keys rattled and the door opened. 'Christ, what a mess. Are you sure it's meningitis?'

'I'm certain, and if he doesn't have treatment, now, he'll die.'

'All right.' He sent the other officer who'd just arrived to call the prison doctor.

By the time the doctor arrived ten minutes later, Petru was visibly worse. He'd vomited again although he was barely conscious, and the rash had spread. The doctor quickly examined him.

'Any other symptoms?' he asked Fraser.

'He's Kernig's sign positive,' Fraser said, pointing to Petru's leg.

'So he is. It's meningococcal meningitis all right — call an ambulance,' he said to one of the officers, who sped away. 'I hope to God we're in time . . . ' He filled a syringe with penicillin as he spoke, injected it straight into a vein, then followed it with another of sulphonamide. Then he turned to Fraser. 'Have either of you two got any symptoms?'

Fraser looked at Ilie, then shook his head.

'Better take these to be on the safe side.' He gave them some sulphonamide tablets.

The officer came back. 'It's on its way,' he said.

'Good. Now we'd better check all the others . . . '

Petru was taken away quickly, but it was nearly two hours before all the other prisoners on the wing were checked and Fraser and Ilie had cleaned up the cell.

Fraser tried to phone Frances in the morning, but no sooner had he reached the phone than Sutton appeared.

'Piss off,' he said to Fraser as he picked up the phone.

With clenched jaw, Fraser did as he was told. Sutton waited until he was out of sight before handing the phone to the next man.

Fraser was worried the same thing would happen in the evening and was going to ask someone to phone Frances for him when the news reached him that Sutton wouldn't be bothering him for a while. He'd gone down with meningitis and had been taken to hospital. He was the only other person on the ship to get it.

That evening, Humber sauntered past Fraser. 'How the hell did you do it?' he murmured and went on his way.

All round the ship, people looked at him with respect, even awe. He decided not to enlighten them.

Both Petru and Sutton recovered quickly and were back after a few days. Petru was pathetically grateful and couldn't do enough for him. Sutton left him alone.

18

The English of the two Romanians, especially Ilie's, improved dramatically with Fraser's help, and after a game of chess one evening, he told Fraser their story.

They'd been born in the same village about fifty miles from Bucharest and their parents had been peasant farmers, impoverished, but not unhappy. Then, when the boys were ten, Ceausescu's master plan had been unveiled. One morning, the police had herded the entire population into temporary huts while the bull-dozers razed every building to the ground.

'Even the church,' Ilie said, his face twisted with hatred.

'Are you religious?' Fraser asked.

'No, but my mother and father were. And my mother's mother and father — it kill them.'

High-rise blocks of flats were jerry built over the ruins and the villagers forced to live in them.

'Petru,' Ilie said, indicating him with a thumb, 'they make him help build.'

'What was your house like,' Fraser asked, 'before that?'

'Small. Very small, but better than flats.'

There was no work for them in the new order; after a while, their parents could no longer afford to feed them and the boys were forced to move to Bucharest. They found work and tried to send money to their families, but things got worse and worse and one bad winter, all their families except Petru's mother died.

Then came the coup and Ceausescu was deposed and shot.

'Nothing change,' said Petru darkly. 'Should have shot *all* . . . '

'Same people rule us,' said Ilie.

They'd tried going home, but there were still only the bleak flats and no work. Even when the regime became more liberal, it was still difficult to earn more than enough for the basic necessities.

Then Petru's mother had died. When he went through her effects, he found a gold pendant, a family heirloom he hadn't known existed. Normally, the state would have confiscated it, but Ilie had black market contacts, so they sold it and decided to use the money to come to Britain.

'Why Britain?' Fraser asked.

'Is most . . . generos . . . ?'

'Generous,' Fraser said. 'Liberal.'

'*Da*! Yes.'

They'd been transported across Europe in a succession of old trucks and even older vans, usually with groups of gypsies. Ilie spoke the word with undisguised contempt — non-judgemental principles were evidently a concept unknown to him.

In France, they were sewn into the canvas sides of freight wagons bound for Britain through the Channel Tunnel.

'Oh, come on,' Fraser said in disbelief.

'Is true! Is true!'

'What about food?'

'No food, little water only. No want piss.'

'How long were you in there?'

'Two, three day.'

They'd suffered cold to the point of hypothermia during the actual journey, then they'd been shunted into a marshalling yard and left. They'd waited till dark before cutting their way through the ceiling of the wagon. Petru had gone first, reaching for the cable conveniently placed overhead only to find it was electrified and badly burning his hands. He held them up now for Fraser to see — they were still scarred.

They'd had no idea of what to do or where to go, and before long they were both arrested. This was just as well in some ways; Petru couldn't have gone on much longer and, as it was, he had to stay in hospital for a week.

Their pleas for asylum had been turned down and they were charged with illegal immigration. They were offered better terms for informing on the people who'd brought them over, but the organisation had covered their trail too well.

'Is fuck up,' said Petru, a man of few words.

'Do we have chance at trial?' Ilie asked Fraser.

'I don't know. I'll ask my lawyer if you like.'

He asked Agnes, who said they'd almost certainly be found guilty and then either deported immediately, or imprisoned for a few months first. Either way, they'd end up back in Romania.

★   ★   ★

The bolt fell the following week.

At visiting time, Mary wouldn't meet his eyes. Her own were red and swollen.

'What is it, Mary, what's happened?'

'Oh Fraser, she's relapsed. She's really ill and I don't know what's going to . . . ' She began crying while Fraser sat stunned. He remembered now that Frances had seemed distracted on the phone the evening before but, wrapped in his own problems, he hadn't really paid attention at the time. He reached out and covered Mary's hands with his.

'Have you spoken to Dr Saunders?'

'Yes . . . ' She gathered herself up and dabbed at her eyes with a tissue. 'He says they're going to stabilise her, get her into remission again and then go for a marrow transplant.' She told him how they'd already taken blood from her for matching and that Frances' brother in Africa was flying over. 'Fraser, what are her chances?'

About ten per cent . . . 'There are so many variables,' he prevaricated, 'It's completely unpredictable.'

'That's what Dr Saunders told me. Fraser, she needs you more than anything — is it possible for you to come?'

'I'll put in an application as soon as you've gone.'

Which he did.

Ilie asked him later what was wrong and Fraser told him just that Frances wasn't too well.

Ten per cent. One in ten. The numbers went round and round his head . . . He *had* to see her . . .

He was called to the governor's office the next day. He knew as soon as he saw his face that it was bad news.

'Dr Callan, I'm afraid I have to turn down

242

your request for leave of absence.'

'*Why?*' It came out as a whisper.

'It's our policy here always to take advice from the police, and they are adamant in this case that you shouldn't be given leave. This is partly because of the nature of the crime you've been accused of, but also because of the fact that you showed violence when you tried to escape arrest. You've also been involved in violence since you've been here. I'm sorry.'

Fraser tried to gather his wits. 'Sir . . . my fiancée is almost certainly dying and if I — '

'Oh come, that's rather defeatist, isn't it? You said in your application that they're arranging a transplant.'

'Sir, I am a doctor and I'm telling you that her chances are around ten per cent. She could die while I'm stuck in here . . . I beg you . . . '

'My hands are tied. I'm sorry.'

Fraser shouted, 'You *have* to let me go!'

'There's no have to about it, Callan.' The governor seemed almost relieved to have the argument out in the open. 'The answer's no and that's all there is to it.' He glanced at the prison officer. 'I don't think there's any point in continuing this discussion.'

The officer took Fraser's arm. He shook it off and balled his fists —

'Now, don't be stupid, Callan.'

For a wild moment, Fraser thought about smashing his fists into the officer's face, then something inside him collapsed and he allowed himself to be led away.

He walked like an automaton, like a man being led to his execution. There were no thoughts in his brain, only the dimmest of existences . . .

'You stay here for a bit,' the officer said, not unkindly, when they were back in his cell. He patted his shoulder and left. Fraser sank on to Petru's bed and sat, not moving.

Time passed unheeded.

He dimly realised Ilie and Petru had returned.

'Hi, Fraser.' Ilie. 'Hey, sumthin' wrong, man?' He sat down beside him.

Fraser, watching himself in utter astonishment, began to cry. Just tears at first, then snivels, then sobs that reached down into his soul . . .

Ilie had an arm round him. There was a noise at the door, then a laugh — it was one of the other Romanians.

'Hey! *Copil de tata!*'

In a flash, Petru turned and sank his fist deep into the other's gut. The breath whistled out of him as he sank to his knees clutching his belly. Petru let out a stream of Romanian and the winded man's companion dragged him away.

Petru shut the door and the two of them waited while Fraser cried himself out. Then they listened.

The next day Agnes visited him.

'I'm so sorry, Fraser. I've been to see Garrett, but there's no moving him. I'm going to see whether there are any legal moves I can make.'

For two days, Frances was too ill to speak to him much, then she recovered a little. Agnes wrote to tell him there was no legal way she could force leave, but she was going to try appealing above Garrett's head. Fraser, who'd recovered some of his stony composure, told the others.

'Is simple,' said Ilie after receiving a nod from Petru. He lowered his voice. 'Fraser, we have plan. We give you, we help you escape.'

★　★　★

Tom paused at the ward entrance, then pressed his lips together and went in.

'I've come to see Miss Templeton,' he told the sister.

She'd asked him to come and he felt obliged to, although he didn't know how he could help. He and Agnes had been working on the problem of tracing the shares and got absolutely nowhere — the size of the market, the sheer numbers of them that passed hands every day defeated them.

He assured the sister he hadn't got any infectious illnesses he knew of and went in.

'Hello, Mr Jones. Thank you for coming.'

For a moment he didn't recognise her. Her face was a dull yellow and her eyes were sunken in bruised sockets. Drips fed into both her arms.

'It's the least I could do,' he said.

'As you can see, I've relapsed.' Her voice at least was unchanged. 'They're talking about giving me a transplant but the chances of success are about one in ten. I've probably got a few months left, but I could die at any time. I want to see Fraser before . . . ' Her eyes closed briefly and when she opened them again they were very bright.

'I want to see Fraser and they won't let him come.' She explained what had happened and he listened, although he already knew most of it from Agnes. 'Can you help, please, Mr Jones?'

'In what way?'

'By putting pressure on the police — I thought your department had some influence.'

'I'm afraid the police have more in this case

'— you know that they're behind it?'

She nodded.

'I'll talk to Agnes and see what legal options we have, then I'll go and talk to the police.'

'Tell them they can ask Dr Saunders, he'll tell them how ill I am.'

'I'll try, but please don't hold out too much hope.'

'I *have* to hope,' she said with intensity, 'The thought of dying without seeing Fraser again is more than I can bear.'

He said, 'Don't talk yourself into dying, Frances, ten per cent chances do come off.'

'Oh yeah?'

'D'you have many relatives still around?'

'Dozens.'

'Well, it could be better than ten per cent then, one of them's probably going to be a match for you.'

'You're an expert on marrow transplant, are you?' she flashed.

'No, but my wife works in a haematology lab.'

'I'm sorry,' she said. 'That was inexcusable.'

'It's all right.'

After a pause, she said, 'I can accept dying, I suppose. I can accept that this has happened to me, although I find myself wondering, Why me, why now?'

'You wouldn't be human if you didn't.' He realised that she desperately needed someone to talk to and tacitly volunteered.

'I don't *want* to die, I'm scared of dying . . . Having Fraser with me would make it easier to bear.'

'I promise you we'll do our best.'

She continued as though he hadn't spoken: 'You know they say that few relationships can survive a serious illness — well, ours would — *will*, I mean. I have absolute faith in Fraser, I'm lucky in that. He's the only thing I do have any faith in — other than my mother and brother, I suppose.' The words came tumbling faster. 'I've got no religious faith. Sometimes I wish I had, but I'm a biologist . . . I read somewhere once that of all scientists, biologists are the least likely to have any . . . I suppose it's because we know how the human body works and that when it's gone, it's gone. When Descartes said, 'I think, therefore I am,' he forgot to add, 'I think with my brain and when my brain ceases to think, I cease to be' . . . Perhaps I should have been a philosopher . . . '

She ran on and Tom listened. After a while, she said, 'I'm imposing on you, going on like this.'

He shook his head. 'Not at all.'

'Why am I telling you?'

He smiled. 'Sometimes it's easier revealing yourself to a stranger.' He didn't add that people, especially women, often did tell him things.

She smiled back as though he had. 'Perhaps you should have been a Samaritan rather than an investigator.'

'I'd have probably been one of the bad sort.'

'Yes, you probably would,' she said, looking at him slightly askance. 'Does your wife have faith in you, I wonder?'

'That, I couldn't say.'

'You said she's a biologist like me. Does she believe in anything? — I'm sorry, that's an impertinence.'

'She believes the same as me — in something, but we don't know what.'

'You must have some idea . . . a deity?'

For a moment, Tom's eyes were far, far away, then he shook his head. 'You don't want to know . . . '

'How do you know? I might.'

He said slowly, 'I had a near death experience once — at least, I assume that's what it was — when I was twenty . . . '

'Go on.'

'I was in the army, believe it or not. Some of us were horsing round in the gym and it got a bit rough. Someone got an armlock around my throat and I passed out. They couldn't bring me round and the poor sod thought I was dead . . .

'Well, I wasn't. I was in another place, a fantastic place. All I can remember is that it was green and there were trees and water and other people and I was happy. I didn't realise how happy until there was this pain in my leg and I realised I was being pulled back — back here, that is. I remember begging, pleading, screaming with rage because I *did not want* to come back. God, I didn't. But come back I did. The pain in my leg was because it was doubled up under me . . . ' He smiled. 'The bloke who'd done it was pleased to see me back, though.'

After a pause, she said, 'I'm not surprised. How long were you out?'

'Only a few minutes. I know you'll say it was all in the mind and I can't prove it wasn't, but it was real enough to me at the time.'

'I wouldn't presume to tell you anything.'

'You see, three years ago, my brother died. He was a haemophiliac and he had AIDS. He was all the family I had and I rather like to think of him being in that other place.'

She said gently, 'Let's hope he is.'

19

There were times when Tom hated the police. He'd been a copper himself for ten years before working for Marcus and had been reasonably happy, but now he was reminded of everything he disliked about them. Just some of them, he told himself.

After leaving Frances, he'd phoned Marcus, who'd told him there was nothing he could do officially about Fraser.

'Your best bet is to try and persuade Garrett face to face. Get him to check on Miss Templeton's condition himself — when he realises how ill she is, he might change his mind.'

'Wouldn't that be better coming from you, Marcus?'

'I don't think so, Tom. You're closer to the situation than me, and prisons are one area I don't have much influence in.'

Tom went to see Agnes again (any excuse) and she told him much the same thing.

'It's one of those areas where the discretion of the prison governor *is* in effect the law.' She thought for a moment. 'We could try and get Fraser's MP to take it to the Home

251

Office, or maybe even try the Ombudsman, but it all takes time . . . '

So there was nothing for it but to go and try Garrett.

He agreed to see Tom, listened patiently to what he had to say and then said, 'I'm sorry, Mr Jones, but the answer's no. He's been charged with a very nasty murder, and he offered violence to my officers when they tried to arrest him, inflicting grievous bodily harm to one of them in the process.'

'But that wouldn't have happened if it weren't for his fiancée's illness — '

'I dare say a lot of things wouldn't have happened if it weren't for his fiancée's illness. Dr Flint would still be alive for one, and my officer wouldn't have a fractured jaw for another. Besides which, he's under suspicion for murdering Dr Somersby as well.'

'Do you have any evidence for that?'

'Not yet, I'm still looking.'

Tom said, 'Can't you at least check for yourself on how ill his fiancée is?'

'I don't need to, Mr Jones. I accept everything you say about her and I'm very sorry, but the fact remains that Callan is, in my opinion, too dangerous a man to allow out of prison.'

And that was that. *It's only some of them,* Tom reminded himself as he left.

★ ★ ★

Fraser, meanwhile, was making preparations.

'I need a flat piece of metal an inch wide and about a foot long, with a hook on the end — like this . . . ' He drew it for them.

'Problem,' said Ilie. 'If metal, go bleep . . . ' He indicated something around himself with his arms.

'Metal detector?'

'*Da*! I make in plastic?'

Fraser thought for a moment. 'Yeah, so long as it's stiff. I need another piece of plastic too, like a credit card . . . ' He drew that for them.

'No problem.'

'A lock pick? A nail would probably do.'

Ilie looked at Petru, then said, 'Maybe we find one somewhere.'

'A screwdriver?'

'Two problem — metal detector, an' they check stuff after class, count them.'

Petru said something in Romanian. Ilie listened, then said, 'We gonna need metal cutter anyway for fence, we have to steal it.' He paused, then said, 'If we do this, they close machine shop, men not like us after that.'

Fraser pressed his lips together, aware of how much they were doing for him.

253

Reading him, Ilie said, 'Is OK, Fraser. When you get out, you help us stay in Britain, *da?*'

'I'll do everything I can,' Fraser promised, thinking, *Poor naïve bastards, what chance have I got . . . ?*

He spent every minute he could in the exercise yard on top of the ship, watching the comings and goings of all the boats and their owners. He studied the wharf itself and the people who worked round the quayside.

He chatted up prison officers, different ones each time, trying to find out the dimensions of the Derwent, the depth of water, the tides.

He went to the gym every day, trying to keep fit and practising his breathing. And he sat, thinking, going over each move, each permutation.

He phoned Frances every evening and was relieved that she sounded a little better — no worse, anyway. He knew that if he succeeded in escaping, it would damn him even further with the authorities, but when Agnes told him about the failure of Tom's latest efforts, he told himself he had nothing to lose.

★   ★   ★

Tuesday morning, the English class ... The teacher was to recall later that the three of them seemed somehow preoccupied.

Lunch. Ilie and Petru ate a little, Fraser nothing at all. Then the two Romanians went to the machine shop for their class while Fraser went back to his cell. The temptation to check that the plastic tools were still in their hiding places was almost overwhelming, but he resisted — fortunately, since a party of prison officers descended without warning for a spot search.

After they'd gone, he sat on Petru's bed and tried to make himself relax, breathing in and sighing out to stimulate the endorphins ... *Just one chance*, he thought, *but what have I got to lose ... ?*

★   ★   ★

Petru sauntered through the metal detector, but as Ilie followed it emitted a high-pitched bleeping. He was grabbed by a couple of prison officers as he bumped into Petru.

'Hold it, everyone,' said one of them. He began patting Ilie down and almost immediately found the pair of pliers in his pocket.

'You stupid berk,' he said, holding them up. Ilie just shrugged.

'It might be a blind,' said the other. 'I think

we should strip search him.'

They finished patting him down, then took him to one side and made him strip. The Stanley knife was in his underpants.

'If you want castrating,' said the first officer, brandishing it in his face, 'You just ask us and we'll do it for you.'

'One more caper like this, sunshine,' said the other, 'an' you'll be in front of the governor . . . ' They told them all to go. Petru didn't take out the metal cutters that Ilie had slipped into his pocket until they'd joined Fraser in the cell.

Fraser quickly packed his wash-bag and suspended it from his waist so that it hung inside his trousers.

'You look like you need good fuck up,' observed Petru, and the others giggled nervously.

They made their way up to the yard, Fraser trying to keep between them. The sun blazed down, striking diamonds from the wave tops. *Good news, and bad news . . .*

They walked slowly round the perimeter, pretending to talk, watched by three officers. Gulls wailed. Fraser took off his shirt. They reached the point where Petru had spotted the weakness in the fence and Fraser knelt down, loosened his shoelaces, stood up again. He breathed deeply — in, out . . . in, out . . .

The yard filled. The screws chatted amiably with some of the prisoners, their eyes ceaselessly flicking round the rest.

'OK, Fraser?' murmured Ilie.

'OK.' His heartbeats were threatening to spew over into his lungs and he could barely speak.

Ilie gave a nod, and their two countrymen on the other side of the yard started shouting at each other . . . then one of them threw a punch.

The screws ran over, trying to force their way through the ring of men already forming.

Petru whipped out the cutters and ducked under the bar. He cut down to the deck where the fence had rusted, then upwards, attacking the flat metal between the oblong holes — snip, snip, snip — moving smoothly up like a can opener . . .

Once he'd cut to his height, he lashed with his foot, tearing the fencing away from the deck. He bent it outwards, then began kicking the other side, and that's when the screw saw him —

'Hey!'

He began running over, but a deftly placed foot tripped him and he sprawled on to the deck as the other two officers struggled to free themselves from the jostling crowd.

Petru pushed the other side of the fence

257

out, Fraser kicked off his shoes and ducked through, Petru followed, and then Ilie, but he was grabbed by a screw before he could make it . . .

Ilie did his best to delay the screws, blocking the hole so that they couldn't get after the others . . . Petru danced noisily towards the bow while Fraser worked his way quietly sternwards . . . Then he pulled off his trousers, heaving in deep breaths.

He took a step back, filled his lungs with air once more, then leaped out as far as he could to avoid hitting the slanting sides of the ship . . . and the last thing he heard as the air whipped past him was the mewling of the gulls . . .

Ilie was yanked aside, his hands streaming blood where he'd gripped the fence, and the officer ducked through.

'Come on, lad, don't be a fool.' He was talking to Petru, a few feet away.

Petru jabbered at him in Romanian, walking backwards, enticing him to follow . . . When he could go no further, he too jumped outwards, emitting a primal scream as he fell through the air.

'Man overboard, port side,' another screw shouted into his mobile. They watched as Petru surfaced and began swimming away from the boat.

The siren began to wail.

Below, three more officers pulled on life-jackets and jumped into the launch.

'Ready?' the one in charge, who was called Kevin, shouted.

He pulled a cord and the boat fell horizontally into the water. The motor started first time and the man at the helm steered her round.

'There he is!'

Petru's head bobbed in the sea in front of them. He looked round, saw them coming, waited . . . and just before they reached him, he duck-dived and they overshot.

'There, over there!'

They hauled the boat round, but again Petru ducked, and then again . . . but after that, he knew he'd had enough. He allowed them to grab him and haul him over the side like a drowned sheep.

'Are you all right, you dumb bastard?' one of them asked as they turned back to the ship.

The radio crackled.

'It's all right, we've got him and he's OK . . . Oh, *shit*.'

He turned to the others. 'They think there were two of them . . . '

They searched along the side of the ship and along the wharf, then they checked under the stern, and then they searched the other side of the ship and the wharf there.

'Nothing,' Kevin said into the radio.

'You sure?'

'Course I'm fuckin' sure,' Kevin snapped, then paused.

'Better get a diver out, I suppose.'

20

It took Fraser just over a second to reach the
sea, a long, long second in which he felt as
though his whole body was trembling like a
leaf . . . *Hold it straight, hold nose, head up
to avoid a smack in the face . . .*

As he hit the water, some of the breath was
driven out of his body by the shock. He had
no idea how deep he was. *Can't go up . . .* He
turned in the water and swam downwards.
He could see the sun dappling the sandy
bottom as he reached it, levelled off and
turned determinedly for the cliff-like blackness of the ship's hull . . . *Only 120 feet,
that's all . . .*

As he passed into its shadow, he became
aware of the washbag banging into his groin
with each frog stroke of his legs. Was it
slowing him down? *Keep going . . .*

No light now, only blackness and the
sensation of water streaming over his face and
body. *Just keep going . . .*

Without warning, his back scraped into the
hull. He turned down, kicking against it, then
his face hit the sea-bed.

Christ! How much room . . . ?

Keep going.

With a knock, his head hit something. He felt at it — it had to be the keel . . .

He pulled himself under, his heels scraping the sand, his lungs vainly trying to pump as the carbon dioxide level rose in his blood.

An' I'm only half feckin' way . . .

He twisted, got his feet against the keel and heaved. His ears hissed as the sea water streamed past them. He could feel his diaphragm pulling at his lungs now, heaving at them, trying to force them to work.

Light! Ahead . . .

His joints began fizzing — elbows, shoulders, hips, knees — like pins and needles as he willed his muscles to keep working, keep forcing him through the water . . .

Light . . . His mind began to sideslip. Was it lactic acid causing the pain in his joints, oxygen debt?

Light — a sheet of it above . . . He turned upwards, pulling himself up, up, up towards it.

His head broke surface and his lungs began working like bellows. He could hear as well as feel the air hissing raggedly through his throat — *in out, in out* — couldn't get it quickly enough. He gagged, coughed as he sucked in sea water, pumped his legs to keep his head above the waves.

Sinking, need something to hang on to . . . But there wasn't anything except the slap slap slap of the waves against the side.

A hole, four feet away . . . He kicked towards it, thrust in his fingers and held on.

In out, in out, in out . . . He became aware of the siren again. Had they got the launch out yet? Should he use the tube in his wash-bag? *Not yet, better move* . . . Where, where?

His lungs were working more evenly now . . . *Move along the side of the ship? Swim across to the wharf?*

No. Have to go under again . . .

He kept his lungs working as he tried to measure the distance across to the wharf . . . fifty, sixty feet? Seventy if he went at an angle away from the ship.

Move . . . *I don't want to* . . . *move, move* . . .

He sucked in a last breath and duck-dived, pushing himself off and under from the ship. The sea bottom shifted like a kaleidoscope in the sunlight. Would they be able to see him against it from above?

Depends. Depends how rough the surface is, on whether anyone's looking — had Petru managed the decoy? His lungs started heaving again. *Daren't surface now, bound to see me . . .*

The gloom of the wharf loomed suddenly and he surfaced beside it, grabbed at the weedy timbers and tried to pull himself into the overhang as his lungs worked overtime to try and make up the deficit . . . The siren was still going, he realised as he twisted round in the water to look.

The sun glinted on the windows in the side of the ship — were there people watching him from behind them even now? He could see the fencing of the yard at the top, but no figures behind it.

Better turn to hide the whiteness of his face . . . *Time to use the tube? Not yet . . .*

He began slowly working along the wharf, keeping his back to the sea. It was stinging now, his back, as the salt got to work on the abrasions, and he wondered how bad it was.

A whine pierced the wail of the siren and he glanced over his shoulder to see the launch swinging round the stern of the ship.

Go under, where's the tube, go under . . .

No. He was only twenty feet from his target and they were searching the side of the ship — *swim, swim* — fifteen feet, ten . . . He could see the name of the motor boat now, *Omen . . . Good or bad?* Then he'd reached the stern and hung to its rudder, hiding behind it.

He could stay here in the water indefinitely, although sooner or later they'd search . . . and the cold was already leaching the warmth from his body.

But if he climbed over the stern, they'd see the whiteness of his body, and if he swam to the bow, he'd still have to work his way back to the stern . . . and be seen . . .

But maybe he could worm his way along the decking — There was suddenly the strangest silence as the siren fell away to be replaced, very gradually, by the wailing of the gulls . . . It was time to move.

He breathed deeply again — only twenty feet this time. He pushed himself under and swam the length of the boat and surfaced by the bow. He reached up, his fingers went round the chain and he tried to pull himself up . . . but he hadn't realised how weak the diving had made him.

More deep breaths, then he gritted his teeth and willed his arms to flex . . . an elbow on the deck, then the other on the wharf . . . and the sea reluctantly gave him up.

He lay in the sun on the hot deck . . . *Move, they might be here any minute* . . .

He lifted himself on to elbows and knees and inched himself along, trying to keep below the line of the wharf . . . ten feet, five, then he fell in a heap into the well of the stern.

He listened, no shouts, looked at the cabin door — *Oh thank you, God*. A simple Yale lock. He fumbled in the wash-bag, found the plastic card and thrust it through the crack against the tongue and pushed — with a snick, the door swung open. He slipped through and shut it behind him.

His eyes adjusted and he saw he was in a tiny kitchen. He shivered violently as he realised how cold he was . . . His feet slapped wetly as he made his way through a lounge-cum-bedroom to an even smaller room with a basin . . . and a towel!

He snatched it, pulled off the wash-bag and his sodden underpants and began rubbing himself, wincing as the towel rubbed his injured back.

Still shivering, he went back to the kitchen where he rummaged through the cupboards until he found what he was looking for — the overalls he'd seen the owner wearing, and also an old pair of shoes, laid on top of a toolbox. He pulled them on and immediately felt better.

Back to the basin, where he took out the nail scissors from the bag and began hacking at his beard . . .

Was it worth the risk? They'd be searching here before too long . . . Yes, if it changed his appearance, it was worth it.

When he'd got off as much as he could, he soaped his face and started work with the razor. It felt like a scouring pad and he cut himself repeatedly but at last it was done and a face he hadn't seen for at least ten years peered blearily back at him from the mirror.

Engine next, or the chain . . . ?

The engine — if he was seen working on the chain, he might have to make a quick getaway. He took the toolbox up to the well of the boat . . . looked round, couldn't see anyone, turned to the control board.

It was plastic, fairly simple, the fascia held in by screws. Screwdriver . . . He found one in the toolbox and the screws came out easily.

He pondered the wires . . . *That's the ignition and that one must go to the starter* . . . He pulled them off with pliers, made some connections and then touched . . . The engine turned over a few times and then caught. *Great!* He switched off. Now for the hardest bit.

He found his lock pick and took that and the toolbox up to the bow, his back pricking with pain both real and imagined. The chain passed through a large iron ring on the quay and then through the rail of the boat — *Shit!*

There wasn't a ring on the deck he could unscrew, it would have to be either the lock or the chain.

One attempt with the pliers was enough to tell him that the chain was too tough for them to cut through. And the lock was solid and completely resisted his crude pick.

Could he cut them? He rummaged through the tools for a hack-saw, but couldn't find one . . .

He fell back on his heels as sickness congealed over him . . . To have come so far . . . *Oh fuck, fuck, fuck.*

Oh Frances . . .

Run for it?

He'd be caught.

He looked at the rail again . . . The chain went round it just above the foot, which was held on to the deck with four big screws. Could it be bent upwards?

Gotta try . . .

He took out the biggest screwdriver and started. Two of the screws came easily, one with difficulty, and the last not at all.

He tried leaning on the screwdriver, but the slot was frayed now and the end just slipped over it.

He found a hammer and, after another nervous look round, placed the screwdriver in the slot and banged down several times. Then he placed both hands round the handle, pushed downwards and tried to force his hands round . . . it felt as though the skin was being torn from his palms . . . the screw moved a millimetre . . . another . . . then it was free.

He looked at the rail again. There was only one way the foot could move — up, so he took the hammer and bashed upwards. The rail slowly bent and the foot raised itself an inch from the deck. He pulled on the chain to get some slack, then slipped it under and it fell with a plop into the sea.

The stern was held on with rope, which he cut with a kitchen knife and hauled aboard, then he started the engine again.

Fraser had never conned a boat before in his life. He looked at the controls. A wheel — for steering. A lever marked *Throttle* — fair enough . . . *Drive* one way and *Reverse* another.

The stern was sticking out more than the bow, so he cautiously put the throttle into reverse — and with a clunk, the engine note dropped and the boat edged slowly backwards.

Magic! When he judged he was far enough out, he switched the throttle to drive and gingerly opened it — and the boat moved forwards.

He spun the wheel and headed out to sea.

★ ★ ★

While the diver was being called, a party of prison officers began searching the quay and all the boats on the port side of the ship.

After a while, Kevin suggested that, for form's sake, a couple of them should search the seaward side as well, and Darren and Andy were dispatched.

There wasn't a great deal to search.

'We'd better ask Ol' Man Bailey if he's seen anything,' Andy said.

'Is he here this afternoon, then?'

But as they approached the *Omen*, they saw it turn and head away from them. The figure in the wheel-house gave them a wave and Andy waved back.

270

21

The governor was convinced that the diver would find Fraser's body underneath the ship, and when he didn't, went into overdrive to try and make up for the lost time. The police were informed of the escape and prison officers with dogs were sent to block all the main roads, especially the causeway, and to watch the local railway and bus stations. Ilie and Petru were questioned, but only shrugged their shoulders and muttered in Romanian.

Then Andy got to remembering what a miserable bastard Old Man Bailey was, how he'd never waved or made any friendly gesture to any of them before, and after agonising for five minutes, found Kevin and owned up.

★   ★   ★

Fraser was vaguely aware that Weymouth had a harbour and pointed *Omen* at roughly where he thought it would be. He was making about seven knots, although he wasn't to know that. Gulls cried and circled the boat, hoping for fish. The sun warmed his back and a fine spray from the bow wash found its way into his lungs, and he had to remind himself that this was not the end of his troubles, only another beginning . . .

Do they know I've got the boat yet?

Would they be waiting for him at the harbour, should he ditch *Omen* before he got there?

But if he just left her somewhere, it would look odd, it would be remembered, and he'd still have to walk into town . . . He kept going.

A few minutes later, he picked out the funnel of the cross-Channel ferry and steered for it, and a little over half an hour after he'd started, he reduced throttle as he entered the River Wey. Without thinking about it, he kept to the left of the channel and couldn't understand why the boats coming the other way hooted, one salty dog even shaking his fist at him — then someone shouted, 'You're on the wrong bloody side, man,' and he quickly moved over.

He entered a pool where mostly larger boats were moored. The smaller vessels and sailing craft seemed to be beyond a low swing bridge over which ran a road, but he couldn't see how to get through. He looked round — there was a quay to his left, but all the mooring spaces were taken. Other boats were moored to buoys. Aware that he'd look conspicuous if he hung around for much longer, he steered for the quay and put *Omen* into neutral as he came alongside a large cruiser.

'Anybody there?' he called out.

No answer.

He tied the bow to the cruiser, then went below and packed his wash-bag into the toolbox.

Then, as an afterthought, he went to the basin and carefully cleared away all the hair he could find — no need to let them know he'd shaved off his beard. *Though they've probably already guessed . . .*

Then he picked up the toolbox (camouflage), pulled shut the door, and with a muttered 'Thanks, *Omen*,' climbed on to the cruiser and thence to the quay. He crossed the bridge and headed for town.

Kevin found *Omen* half an hour later.

Fraser was looking for two things: a car-park, and a building site. There were several of the former but none of the latter . . . *Doesn't anybody build anything in Weymouth any more?*

Then he came across a tall building which was being cleaned. He could see two men working above him on the scaffolding. Loose pieces of tubing lay on the pavement . . . To ask or to take? Too late, he'd been seen.

''Elp you, mate?'

'Yeah, I'm doing some plumbing round the corner and I need a lever. Can I use one of these a minute?'

The man looked at his mate, who shrugged.

'Awrigh'. 'Ow do we find you?'

'You'll see my van — Johnson, plumbers.'

'Awrigh'.'

'Thanks.'

Fraser picked up a five foot pole and carried it round the corner, then walked quickly to the most promising of the car-parks. The toolbox was dragging at his arm and shoulder now that he couldn't change hands easily; sweat dribbled into his eyes, and when he saw a public loo, he suddenly realised how thirsty he was, but didn't stop because it might look odd . . .

The car-park. Biggish, around two hundred cars. Long stay, Pay and Display . . . He worked his way through, then spotted the kind of thing he was looking for, a beige Montego around ten years old (before all the clever anti-theft stuff) surrounded by other cars. He made his way over and glanced at the ticket . . . two hours to go. *Need longer really, but . . .*

No one around, so he put down the toolbox and took out the flat plastic rod with the hook in the end that Petru had made for him. No reason why plastic shouldn't work as well as metal, he told himself, no reason at all ... He slipped it down through the space between the window and the rubber seal and started feeling around ...

God's sake don't drop it, abort if you can't — Ah! The hook went round the mechanism and he gently pulled ... and with a dull click, the button on the inside of the door came up. He withdrew the bar and opened the door.

A quick look round inside, then he pulled the bonnet release, went out and opened the bonnet to give him some cover.

Back inside — God, it was hot — he put his hand under the steering column, pulled out a sheaf of wires and cut the plastic tie holding them together.

Oh, shit ... Had they changed the colours?

No, here was the ignition ... battery ... starter ... Should he start her up now?

Yes ... He used the pliers to strip the leads, reconnected, touched, and the engine fired, sweet as a little lamb.

Now the awkward bit ...

He put the toolbox on the passenger seat and looked round. Someone was coming straight towards him — a copper? Jacket and tie, well dressed, not a screw . . .

'Problems?'

'Yeah. Think I've got it sorted now, though,' Fraser said, hoping he wouldn't notice the scaffolding pole.

'Good.' The man unlocked the next car, got in and, with a wave, drove off.

Fraser swallowed, raised a hand in reply . . . Anyone else around?

No. He turned the steering wheel until it was against the lock, threaded the pole through the spokes and heaved — and with a crack, the lock gave. He threw the pole in the back, put down the bonnet and drove slowly away.

About five minutes later, trapped in the one-way system, he wound down the window and put on the fan — and that's when he noticed the fuel gauge, just hovering above the red section . . .

But the warning light wasn't on yet . . . so what did that give him? A couple of gallons, maybe sixty miles . . .

The lights changed and the traffic moved again. He turned into another road, a larger one that went along the sea-front. A sign . . . Dorchester, Bournemouth. He saw a space and pulled in.

A uniformed flunkey scurried out from a hotel entrance. 'Can't park here, sir.'

He drove on . . . nothing but hotels, so he turned into a side street. Opened the glove compartment — Ah! An AA handbook. He opened it and found the maps . . .

The main roads would be blocked by now, but what about the B roads? Have to risk it, the minor ones weren't marked here and he didn't have the petrol to spare . . . Head for Dorchester, then go off at —

No. One place they'd certainly have a block would be between here and Dorchester. He studied the map again . . . A B road went along the coast to Bridport, then Broadwindsor, Crewkerne, Somerton — could he get that far?

Gotta try . . .

A few minutes later, as he went over the bridge that divided the harbour, he couldn't help glancing at the *Omen.*

Crawling with uniforms . . .

The shock stole his senses away and for a moment he lost all track of what he was doing or where he was going . . . daren't stop — then he saw a sign for Abbotsbury.

The suburbs seemed to go on for ever and his head began to ache. Another mile, then he saw a phone box and pulled in beside it. Dialled 100 and asked to make a reverse charge call to Mary Templeton.

'Who shall I say is calling?'

'Er — her son-in-law, John Fraser.'

After an interminable time (*Bugged* . . . ? *Can't be, not yet — can it* . . . ?) Mary's voice said, 'Fraser?'

'Have the police told you yet?'

'Told me what?'

'I've escaped, I need help — '

'Oh, Fraser!' she wailed. 'You idiot, you'll make things worse, you must give yourself up — '

'Mary, listen — it's the only way I'll get to see Frances, the only chance I'll have to prove I didn't kill Connie. I need clothes and money. And some paracetamol,' he added, touching his aching head. 'Please, Mary, you're the only chance I've got.'

'What kind of clothes?' she said at last. 'D'you want me to go to your house?'

'No — whatever you do, don't go there. I need everything — socks, pants, shirt, the lot. I'm sorry, you'll have to buy them . . . Marks and Spencer — anything.'

'But I don't even know your size,' she said faintly.

'Shoes nine, thirty-three leg and waist — '

'Wait a minute, let me write it down . . . '

He repeated it while she did so.

'Anything else?' she asked.

He thought a moment. 'Yes, a cassette recorder . . . ' He described exactly what he wanted. 'And some cord.'

'Where shall I bring them?'

'D'you know Glastonbury?'

'Not really.'

'Wells?'

'Only the cathedral.'

'That'll do. Meet me there as soon as you can . . . Leave now before the police get on to you.'

'But Fraser — '

'*Please*, Mary, just go.'

As he put the phone down, he realised he was shaking. Could he trust her, would she tell the police? *Got no choice* . . . He went back to the car. His head was throbbing wickedly now. *Dehydration?*

He drove on. In Abbotsbury, he found a public loo and drank from a tap, his body soaking up the water like sand. He set off again, feeling slightly better — then the fuel light winked on.

Make it to Wells? Gotta try . . .

★ ★ ★

Officers, police and prison, had searched the *Omen* and found nothing.

'Engine's still too hot to touch,' the police sergeant said to Kevin. 'He's not long gone. What d'you think he'll do?' he asked.

'He'll try and get to Avon.'

'Has he got any money?'

'I . . . we don't know.'

After a pause, the sergeant said, 'Well, we've got the trains and buses covered, but if he can do this — indicated Fraser's rewiring — he can do a car.'

'Have you got road blocks up?'

'Major roads, yes. The minor ones we're doing now. He won't get far,' he said, confidently.

The Montego was reported stolen an hour later.

★　★　★

Bridport, Broadwindsor, Crewkerne . . . Fraser tried to go as easy as he could on the petrol, but the roads he'd chosen were all hills and bends . . .

Somerton, then Glastonbury. He glanced at his watch, six thirty, a bit over an hour since he'd phoned Mary, then he saw a sign: Wells three miles. *I'm going to make it*, he thought exultantly. *I'm going to make it* . . .

Ah, hubris . . . The engine coughed, picked up, coughed again and died. He pulled in and stopped.

Three miles . . . She'd probably be there by now. Would she wait? Could he walk it? Take at least forty minutes, probably more.

He got out, pulled the bonnet up again and waited. A car approached, he thumbed vigorously, pointing at the open bonnet. The car swerved to avoid him, drove on. As did the next, and the next . . .

The fourth stopped. 'Broken down?'

'Yeah.' He didn't want to explain why he couldn't buy petrol. 'Can you give me a lift into Wells?'

'Like me to take a look at it?'

And see my wiring? He forced a short laugh. 'I'm a mechanic, an' if I can't fix it, no offence, but I doubt you can. Just a lift, if you wouldn't mind.'

'Sure.' He leaned over, opened the passenger door.

Fraser paused. 'Have you got any plastic for your seat? My overalls . . . '

The man laughed. 'Don't worry about that.'

Fraser climbed in, aware of his gleaming, sockless ankles . . .

'Got far to go?' The driver didn't seem to have noticed them.

'Gloucester.' May as well embroider . . . 'I've got AA relay, so they should get me there all right.'

'Want a lift back when you've phoned them?'

'Oh, that's all right . . . ' *Why d'you only meet nice people when you don't want them?* 'I — er — need to get one or two things in Wells.'

'Suit yourself.'

'Thanks anyway.'

They continued in silence. On the outskirts of Wells, a police car was parked, watching the traffic. Fraser swallowed his heart, tried to stay calm . . . *Probably nothing to do with me. Probably . . .*

'Anywhere particular?'

'Eh? Oh, anywhere near the centre.'

A couple of minutes later, he was dropped in the market square beside a phone booth. He lifted the receiver, waited till the man had gone, then ran across the road to the entrance to the close . . . Mary was sitting on a bench under the west front, smoking a cigarette beneath the disapproving gaze of at least fifty saints.

22

She shrank away as he approached her and he suddenly realised she hadn't recognised him.

'Mary, it's me.'

'Fraser?'

He dropped on to the seat beside her, kissed her cheek. 'Thank you for coming, Mary. Did you get the clothes?'

'Yes. They're in my car.' Still she stared at him.

'Thanks . . . ' He hesitated. 'I think we'd better go. I had to ditch the car outside Wells and the police might find it any minute.'

'What car?'

'I — er — borrowed one.'

Her bemusement turned to resignation as she stubbed out her cigarette and stood up. 'I don't know what you think you can achieve by this, Fraser.'

They started walking. He said, 'You told me yourself that Frances needs me.'

She shook her head. 'Not this way, Fraser . . . '

'And I have an idea of how to prove I didn't kill Connie — did you get the cassette recorder and the other stuff I asked for?'

She nodded. 'It's in the car, through here.' She led him into the square where he'd been dropped a few minutes earlier. 'Over here . . . ' She unlocked the Golf and brought out some bags.

Fraser looked round and saw a Gents. 'I'll change in there.'

'Shirt and tie, jacket, trousers . . . underwear and shoes.'

He took them from her. 'I hope you got a receipt.'

For the first time, she smiled at him — a wan smile, but a smile nevertheless. 'And I've brought you a comb — goodness knows, you need one.'

He locked himself into a cubicle while he changed, then splashed water from the basin over his face and combed his hair — she was right, it needed it, and his face still felt rough . . .

'Well, that's certainly an improvement,' she said as he got into the car and stowed the bags and overalls in the back. 'It's amazing what a tie can do . . . Your face looks sore, though.'

'I'll do something about it later.'

'I've got a first-aid kit with some Germolene.' She opened the glove box and handed it to him. 'There are paracetamols in there too — and I've brought you some food.'

'Thanks, but let's get out of here first.'

'Which way?'

'Avon.'

Once they were out of the tiny city, he swallowed some paracetamol, then rubbed Germolene into his face, wincing as it stung. Then he found the food she'd bought — a pasty, some sandwiches and a drink.

'When did you last eat?' she asked, watching him devour them from the corner of her eye.

'Breakfast, and then not much. Too nervous.'

'You had this planned, then?'

He nodded, his mouth full.

'However did you manage it?'

He swallowed. 'That is a hell of a long story . . . ' He told her briefly and she shook her head again.

'They'll put you in one of those maximum security places when they catch you.'

'I've a few things to do first,' he said. 'Starting with seeing Frances.'

'But won't they be expecting you to do that?' she asked.

'They might, but I'm hoping they're still looking for me in Weymouth at the moment.'

'But they might have posted someone there, it's a terrible risk . . . '

'I've got to try, Mary — you can go ahead

and check for me.'

She let out a groan.

'How is she?' he said quickly, trying to change the subject. 'I'm sorry, I should've asked earlier.'

'Well, she seems a little better. She's had a lot of transfusions and Dr Saunders says he thinks he can induce another remission.'

'D'you know what I'd really like to do?'

She shot him a glance but didn't reply.

'Marry her. Just find some official somewhere and make him marry us.' He sighed. 'Silly, isn't it?'

She sighed. 'It's not silly at all, Fraser.'

They reached Avon and drove to the hospital. He waited impatiently while she went ahead to check. She was back after ten minutes and her face told him the worst.

'There's someone sitting outside her door, I'm sure it's a plainclothes policeman.'

He leaned his head on the steering wheel, hit the rim several times with the palm of his hand . . . then he looked up.

'*Outside* her room?'

'Yes'

'And the door's shut?'

'Of course it is, she's still under barrier nursing — why?'

'The garden, I can get in through the garden. Does she know I'm here?'

'Yes, I had to tell her — Fraser, you *can't* — '

'I *have* to . . . You go back inside and unlock the french window . . . *please*, Mary.'

He gave her five minutes, then walked to the entrance, looking out for any other police . . . down the corridor until he reached the door leading to the little garden . . . a quick look round, then through . . . He could see Mary's face on the other side of the glass.

She opened the window and let him in.

For an instant, he thought they'd come to the wrong place — although he knew what the disease could do, he wasn't prepared for the change in her. Then he realised Frances hadn't recognised him, either.

'Fraser?'

He went over and took her hand, unable to speak. He kissed it, pressed it into his face . . . kissed her mouth, cheeks, eyes . . .

'Oh, you silly man,' she said, 'they'll catch you.'

'I *had* to come — '

'Quiet!' hissed Mary. She went over to the door and listened.

Frances said, 'They'll catch you and I'll never see you again . . . ' Her cheeks were wet.

'You will, I promise you . . . '

She clung to him, eyes closed . . . then at last, she held him at arm's length, looking at him.

'You know,' she said, her voice still shaky, 'I think I preferred you with the beard.'

'Aye, I know,' he said. 'When I looked in the mirror, I remembered why I'd grown it in the first place.'

She smiled, sad-happily. 'It'll grow back.'

And as she smiled, he saw the same unchanging person look out of her eyes.

'Yeah. I couldn't wait that long, though. How're you feeling?'

'Better than last week.'

'I wish I could stay.'

'So do I.'

He left five minutes later.

Frances hadn't known Leo's address, so he tried Directory Enquiries on a phone in the corridor, only to be told that Leo was ex-directory.

So while Mary went to wait in the car, Fraser called the lab to make sure it was empty, then walked quickly up to the door and punched the numbers into the security lock . . . *Please God they haven't changed it . . .*

They hadn't: it clicked and the door swung open. He went through to Ian's office, turned on the light and started looking for an address book . . .

Not on the desk, try the drawers — Ah! He checked Leo's address was in it, then slipped the book into his pocket.

Anything else he could do? No, not enough time . . .

He left as quietly as he'd come, walked out of the main entrance and towards Mary's car — *there were people with her, Agnes and Jones* . . .

He switched direction, aware that Jones had turned round. Mary must have glanced over at him . . . He rounded a corner, started running . . . through a door, into a corridor, and back into the flower shop, from where he could see them . . .

It was all right, they were heading for the main entrance. He watched them go in, then went cautiously back to Mary.

'You saw them?' she gabbled as she drove off. 'God, I thought they'd never go and then you came . . . '

'What did they want?'

'They were going to see Frances.'

'Did they say anything about me?'

'No, nothing.'

'I saw Jones looking round at me, did he — ?'

'I'm sure he didn't recognise you, I'd have known if he had.'

She drove to a taxi rank and got out of the car.

'I hope you know what you're doing, Fraser,' she said.

So do I, he thought as he drove away.

He stopped to look up Leo's road in the A-Z, then drove over to it and past Leo's house. It wasn't dark yet, but the curtains were drawn and he could see a chink of light between them.

He stopped about fifty yards away and switched off the engine. He took a deep breath. Stuffing the cassette player into one pocket and the cord into another, he got out, locked the car and walked to the house. Rang the bell.

As it sounded, it suddenly occurred to him that there might be a chain — too late now . . .

The door opened — no chain — and before Leo could react, Fraser shoved him backwards and followed him in, slamming the door behind him with a foot. Leo staggered against the hall wall, recovered — didn't waste time shouting, just picked up a solid glass ball from a table and flung it at him.

It caught his shoulder, knocking him off balance before falling to the carpet with a thud as Leo charged him head down and caught him in the belly. He fell back winded with Leo on top of him. Leo grabbed the glass ball again and tried to bring it down on his head, but Fraser caught his wrist . . . They struggled, Leo clawing at Fraser's eyes with his free hand, then Fraser heaved his body like a bronco and threw him off.

Leo still had the ball. He swung it at Fraser's head, caught the tip of his nose as he jerked back. The ball flew out of his hand. Fraser swivelled round on his hips, lashed with his right and caught Leo's nose . . . Again, and this time his fist connected with the point of his jaw and he collapsed.

He wasn't completely unconscious though, just groggy.

Fraser flipped him over, tied his wrists with cord, then hauled him to his feet and marched him down the hall to the kitchen, where he tied him to a chair.

Leo's eyes opened and tried to focus. 'What do you want . . . ?' His voice was quavering. 'Money? You can have all I've got here . . .'

Fraser found another chair and sat facing him. 'Do you not know who I am, Leo?'

Leo's eyes widened — he hadn't, but he did now.

'Fraser . . . Oh my God . . . What do you want?'

'The truth.'

'Sure . . . anything . . . '

Fraser rose from his chair, picked up the electric kettle, filled it with water from the tap and plugged it in.

'Wh-what are you doing?' Leo asked.

'Boiling some water.'

'Why . . . ?'

Fraser sat down again and stared at him.

'Frances is in hospital, dying — in part because of the drug *you* pushed on to her while I was away — '

'That's not true, Fraser.'

'D'you think I'd have allowed her to go on it if I'd been here? You pushed it on to Connie and she pushed it on to Frances.'

Behind him, the kettle began to grumble.

'Fraser, honestly, we all thought Alkovin was OK . . . *more* than OK . . . I told you, remember? I told you it could save her life and I meant it.'

'Are you trying to tell me you knew nothing about the side-effects?'

'*Yes* . . . you *know* I didn't, I kept telling you I didn't . . . '

'That's the wrong answer, Leo. Sam Weisman had been saying it, John Somersby knew about it.'

Behind him, the kettle was murmuring . . .

'We thought Weisman was a nutter, we'd done our own tests and found nothing.'

'So you did know about Weisman?'

'Sure. You told Connie when you came back — remember?'

'No, I mean before — you knew before that, *didn't* you?'

'No . . . '

'And then *I* told you that our patients were getting depressed — I produced the evidence and you ignored it.'

'We *didn't* ignore it, we simply didn't think it was significant.'

'That's the wrong answer, Leo.'

Behind him, the kettle clicked itself off as it boiled.

Fraser got up and unplugged it, then filled a jug with cold water and put them both in his reach. Then he sat down again.

'Look at me, Leo, look at my face . . . you're looking at someone with nothing to lose. My fiancée's dying and I'm in prison charged with murder, not even allowed to see her. Nothin' to lose, see? In a minute, if I don't start hearing the truth from you, I'm going to pour this kettle over your legs — '

Leo was shaking his head. 'You wouldn't . . . ' he whispered.

' — and then over your balls.' Fraser paused, continued: 'So, Leo — the truth. Parc-Reed *must* have known about Weisman's results by the time you started pushing the stuff over here . . . right?'

Leo's mouth worked silently and his eyes hunted to and fro . . . then he said. 'All right, yes, we did know about Weisman's results, but we thought he was cracked . . . '

'So what did Parc-Reed do about it?'

'I don't know exactly, but they told me not to worry about it . . . they said it was being taken care of . . . '

'How? How was it being taken care of?'

'I'm not sure . . . pressure on Weisman from our parent company, I believe, pressure on the major journals not to accept his paper.'

'And then when I produced evidence of these side-effects myself, you rubbished them and had me sent away for three months?'

'That was Connie and Ian . . . Yes, all right.'

'Good, Leo.' Fraser brought out the cassette recorder, switched it on and tested it. 'Now, repeat all that for the tape, please.' He held out the microphone.

Leo's eyes went still as his mind worked . . . 'All right,' he said.

'Good,' Fraser said again when he'd finished. 'Next question: how many Parc-Reed shares do you own?'

'Two thousand.'

'Wrong answer, Leo. How many shares do

you, or *have* you owned?'

Leo looked into his eyes, said, 'I've never owned more than two thousand . . . I swear that's the truth.'

Fraser picked up the kettle. 'Sure about that?'

'It's the truth!' Leo's lips clamped shut and he stared mulishly back at him . . .

He doesn't think I will, he's calling my bluff . . .

Do it, gotta do it . . .

He poured a dollop over his right knee —

Leo screamed and bucked backwards, banging his head on the work surface. Fraser grabbed him, pulled him upright and poured some cold water over his knee.

'You *bastard*, you *bastard* . . . ' Leo whimpered.

He's right . . . I'm a doctor . . . I'm supposed to relieve pain, not cause it . . .

Struggling to keep his voice level, he said, 'How many Parc-Reed shares do you or have you owned?'

'Thirty thousand . . . I sold them a week ago.'

'Good. How about Ian Saunders?'

'Thirty thousand.'

'Has he sold them too?'

'Yes.'

'How about Connie?'

'She . . . she never owned any.'

'Wrong answer, Leo . . . ' Fraser reached for the kettle again.

'No, no — I swear it, I offered her some, but she refused.'

'So why was she pushing Alkovin?'

'She thought she could make her name from a paper on it, that's all she was interested in, I swear it.'

Fraser stared at him, his mind whirring . . . *Could be true . . . might explain why she was going to come clean, not so much to lose as the others, why they had to kill her . . .*

'All right. How did you and Ian manage to buy and sell these shares without your names appearing on the public register?'

Leo hesitated and Fraser could understand why. Up until now, everything he'd admitted was deniable, or could be blamed on to Connie and Ian.

'Through a nominee account,' he said at last.

'Who was the broker?'

'I don't know, it was arranged by the company — No-oo!'

Fraser had snatched up the kettle again and held it hovering above his legs . . . 'The name,' he said between his teeth.

'B-Brent Holman.'

'Where are they based?'

'Birmingham.'

'Address?'

Leo gave it and then repeated everything into the tape.

'That's good, Leo,' Fraser said encouragingly. 'We're nearly there now. Just one more question to go — why did you kill Connie?'

Leo closed his eyes, then opened them again. 'Fraser, why are you doing this to me?'

'Why? You *know* why — because I'm banged up in prison while my fiancée's dying . . . So why did you kill Connie, Leo?'

Leo said slowly, 'You know that I didn't kill her.'

'Are you saying it was Ian?'

'No, it wasn't.'

'Wrong answer, Leo.' Fraser picked up the kettle again.

'All right, all *right*,' Leo screeched. 'I killed her . . . Are you happy now? I killed her, I killed her . . . '

Fraser put the kettle down and picked up the tape, but before he could say anything, a voice from the doorway said, 'I think that's enough now.'

He swivelled round to see Tom Jones pointing a pistol at him.

23

Tom had gone back to Avon to interview the managing director of Parc-Reed, who'd been away until now. He hadn't expected much from him and didn't get it, just professional astonishment that anyone could doubt the company's ethical policies. Then he'd called on Agnes to see whether she'd done any better than him in tracing the shares.

'It's ridiculous,' she said, pacing her office. 'We know that they own, or at least, *have* owned them. Somewhere, there must be a record of them . . . some way of finding it . . . '

'The Stock Exchange have told me that there isn't,' said Tom, 'short of approaching every single broker in the land.'

'And even then we wouldn't know whether they were telling the truth. We'd have to hypnotise them all.'

'Might be simpler to hypnotise Farleigh or Saunders,' said Tom.

'If only . . . ' said Agnes.

It was then that her phone had rung and she'd been told about Fraser's escape.

298

'How the hell did he manage that?' said Tom when she passed on the news.

'They're still not quite sure — apparently, he jumped off the top of the ship and stole a motor boat.'

Tom shook his head in reluctant admiration.

'They made me promise to tell them if he contacts me,' she added. Then she said, 'I think I'd better go and tell Frances ... I don't trust the police and I don't want her finding out any other way.'

'Can I come with you?'

'Sure.'

They went back to her house first where her husband, who'd had the afternoon off fishing, had baked some of the trout he'd caught. Then they went to the hospital.

'Isn't that her mother?' Tom said as they walked to the main entrance.

'So it is,' Agnes said, and raised her hand.

She thought a wave was sufficient greeting and felt mildly irritated when Tom insisted on going over to speak to her.

'Hello, Mrs Templeton.'

'Oh ... hello.'

Never could Tom remember having received so unenthusiastic a greeting. 'Have you been to see Frances?' he asked.

'Yes. I'm just about to leave.'

'That's where we're going. How is she?'

'Rather tired, actually . . . in fact, I think the sooner you go and see her the better . . . so that she can get some rest.'

It was at this moment that her eyes flicked over his shoulder. She quickly dragged them back again, but Tom had noticed and glanced round himself in time to see a man change direction . . .

He looked back at Mary. 'I expect you're right,' he said. 'We'll go on up now.'

They said goodbye and walked over to the entrance.

Agnes said, 'She's got a point, you know, perhaps we should leave it for now.'

As soon as they were inside, Tom said, 'She's waiting for Fraser.'

'*What?*'

'I saw him a moment ago, he cleared off as soon as he saw us.'

'Are you sure?'

'He's shaved off his beard, but it *has* to be him. You go up and see Frances, I'm going to follow them.'

'But shouldn't we try — '

'He's seen Frances and I want to know where he's going next.'

'But what about the police?'

'Not yet. Give me your mobile number . . .'

He took it down, then waited out of sight just inside the entrance. One or two people looked at him rather strangely as they came in, but then he saw what he was looking for — the man who'd changed direction . . .

It was him all right. He walked quickly over to Mary's car, nervously looking round, then she opened the door for him and they sped off.

Tom sprinted over to the Cooper, which fortunately wasn't parked too far away, charged out past the No Exit sign, narrowly missing an incoming car, and on to the approach road. There was a Fiesta doing about twenty-five in front of him — he indicated, roared past it and reached the junction just in time to see Mary's car disappear into the distance on the right. He caught up, hung back while Mary was dropped at the taxi rank, then followed Fraser to Leo's house.

He stopped some distance away, watched as Fraser went up to the door and disappeared inside, then released his gun from under the dash and ran up to the house. Listened at the door — nothing . . . Tried peering through the letter box, saw the lighted hall and overturned table, thought he heard voices . . .

Then he'd taken the keys he always carried

from his pocket, selected one and inserted it . . .

The third key he'd tried had turned. He'd eased the door open, slipped through and silently shut it behind him. Taken out his gun and crept up the hall . . .

★ ★ ★

Fraser looked up and said to him now, 'You recognised me, then?'

'Yes.'

Fraser nodded to himself as though he'd known this all along. 'You've heard everything here?'

'Pretty much.'

'Then please — *let me finish it* . . . '

'No . . . !' A strangled cry from Leo.

Tom shook his head. 'He didn't do it.'

'Of course he feckin' did it,' spat Fraser.

'He didn't, and forcing him to say he did will only devalue what you've already found — '

'It wasn't *any* of it true,' Leo said urgently. 'I only said it because of what he was doing to me — '

'I'd shut up if I were you,' Tom said conversationally, 'Or I might just block my ears and go for a smoke in your living-room.' He turned to Fraser. 'Now we've got the

302

name of the broker, we'll be able to trace the shares and — '

'If he didn't kill her, then he knows who did.' Fraser spoke quietly but intensely. 'You've seen for yourself what he's like, if we don't get the truth out of him now, we never will.'

Leo desperately tried to hold Tom's gaze. 'I swear I don't know who killed her.'

'You swore you'd never owned those shares,' Fraser said between his teeth. 'You knew Connie was wavering and that's why you went to her house — to shut her up one way or another. You killed her, drove away and then came back for some reason and found me there. It *has* to be you.'

'You know, he does have a point there,' Tom said to Leo. 'And all those shares do give you a powerful motive.'

Sweat had begun running down Leo's face, he noticed. Strange — he'd heard of it happening, but never actually seen it before.

Leo gathered himself together and tried to speak rationally: 'Yes, I did know she was wavering, she'd told Ian and he asked me to go round and try to persuade her to hang on, but *I did not kill her*. I found *you* there with her, Fraser — you go on about my motive, but yours is a damn sight stronger.'

Fraser thrust his face forward into Leo's.

'Why did you tell Garrett I was still holding the stick when I wasn't?' he demanded.

Leo closed his eyes as though to shut out Fraser's fury. 'I honestly can't remember whether you were holding it or not.' He opened them again. 'I knew you'd done it, so it didn't seem to matter.' He sighed. 'And once I'd said it, Garrett wouldn't let it go.' He looked round at Tom. 'Please let me out of here . . . I agree to all the rest, but I didn't kill her.'

'All right,' said Tom, 'I believe you didn't kill Dr Flint. But what about Dr Somersby?'

'What about him?'

'Don't be funny with me, you're not in the position. Someone killed Somersby and you had the best motive and opportunity for it.'

'I was in London when he was killed, for God's sake. The police did their best to pin it on me and couldn't . . . '

Fraser had got up from the chair and moved a little to one side when Tom started questioning Leo. Now, without warning, he kicked the gun out of Tom's hand.

Tom was caught off balance and fell back. Fraser slogged at his face but Tom saw it coming and twisted his head so that it only glanced, then he jabbed at Fraser's face with his left, and as Fraser raised his hands to defend it, punched him once, hard in the belly with his right . . . and Fraser collapsed on to the floor.

Tom retrieved his gun and knelt beside him. 'Sorry about that,' he said. 'But it really would go better for you if you gave yourself up.'

Leo said, 'What about me?'

Tom pulled Fraser's hands behind his back and snapped on plastic handcuffs, just in case, then went over to Leo and sat down.

'What about you indeed,' he said, pulling out his notebook. 'I think we'll have the name and address of that broker again before anything else.'

He took down the details, then, ignoring Leo's pleas, went over to the phone. He checked the number with Directory Enquiries, rang it and listened to the recorded message before putting the phone down again.

'Well, they certainly exist,' he said to Leo. He called Agnes on her mobile, told her he needed her help and suggested she find a taxi. Then he released Leo, who, after getting the circulation back in his hands, started complaining about his burnt knee.

Fraser, who'd recovered somewhat, suggested something in the medicine cabinet that might help. He looked thoughtfully at Tom.

'Mr Jones, I'll come quietly, but can I ask

for something in return?'

'You're in no position to bargain,' Tom told him. 'But you can ask.'

'D'you still think I killed Connie Flint?'

'No, I don't. But I don't think Farleigh here did either.'

'Then, who?'

'I don't know — yet.'

Fraser hesitated, then said, 'If I give myself up, can I do it at the hospital?'

'You want to see Frances again?'

'I want to marry her.'

Tom's eyebrows shot up. 'I don't know about *that* . . . '

'If you get the hospital chaplain to do it, it'd take less than a minute.'

It was Tom's turn to look thoughtful. 'I'll see what I can do,' he said.

Agnes arrived. Tom told her what had happened and got Leo to repeat his admissions in front of her (a casual remark about putting the kettle on again may have helped) then they tried to work out the best approach to the police.

'It simply wouldn't be possible for them to be married tonight, even if Garrett agreed,' Agnes said. 'For any quick marriage, church or civil, there has to be a special dispensation . . . We could probably get that tomorrow, though . . . ' she added thoughtfully.

She phoned Garrett on her mobile and put Fraser's proposition to him. Garrett flatly refused, but when Agnes pointed out to him how bad he'd look in the press, how bad she could *make* him look, he relented and gave his word.

They took Fraser and Leo to the police station where Fraser gave himself up.

Somewhat to Tom's surprise, Garrett kept his word. Fraser was held overnight at the station and the arrangements were made in the morning. He was then taken to the hospital, where Mary was waiting (Tom had managed to keep her part in Fraser's escape quiet), and the chaplain (Frances had decided she wanted him to do it) performed the ceremony. Tom and Agnes also attended.

It took longer than the minute Fraser had thought, although not much, then he was allowed to kiss Frances before being led away. The bride glowed.

★　★　★

Leo, realising that Brent Holman wouldn't hesitate to hang him out in the breeze to save their own reputation, didn't try to deny buying and selling the Parc-Reed shares. Ian admitted it too (Brent Holman's name in his address book made it hard for him to dispute) but both denied suppressing the truth about Alkovin in order to help the price up. They'd been convinced the drug was safe, they insisted. Both also strenuously denied anything to do with the deaths of either John Somersby or Connie.

Fraser was sent to Parkhurst on the Isle of Wight where at least he had a cell to himself and could phone Frances more easily. He wrote to Ilie and Petru thanking them and hoping they hadn't got into too much trouble. He asked Agnes to act for them, and she said she would.

Tom went back to London where he tried putting all the information he had through HOLMES, the Home Office Large Major Enquiry System. The results were inconclusive. This didn't altogether surprise him, since the system was, as its name suggested, designed for large enquiries with numerous suspects. Then he constructed a flow chart of all the people involved, their motives and movements, but this didn't help much either.

Lateral thinking was called for.

There were, he realised, four questions he needed answers to:

Were John Somersby and Connie Flint killed by the same person?

If so, who benefited from both their deaths?

If not, were the two killings connected, e.g. by Alkovin, or were they entirely separate?

Who, separately, benefited from each of the deaths?

The trouble with lateral thinking, he thought, was that although the answer was so easy and obvious once you'd seen it, seeing it in the first place required . . . well, thinking that was lateral.

What about Terry Stroud? A repressed and probably disturbed man who, if he'd known about Somersby's intentions for him (which he almost certainly had), would have definitely benefited from his death — but from Connie's as well?

Had she somehow found out that he'd killed him . . . ?

What about Charles Flint? Arrogant, irascible, probably short of money — he might have benefited from Connie's death in some way — but from Somersby's as well?

He thought about cars, cars in general, and the type that had been used to kill Somersby in particular, then he went back to Avon to look at some of them. This gave him another idea, which he tested out with the help of Agnes.

He thought about fingerprints, especially all those on the stick that had killed Connie. Again with Agnes' help, he set about acquiring prints from everybody involved, however remotely.

24

They met in Portsmouth and went over in Tom's Cooper. On the ferry, Agnes said, 'I wish it didn't have to be this way.'

'No,' Tom said.

It took less time to drive from Fishbourne to Parkhurst than to get through all the security at the prison, but by midday they were in a glass-walled room with Fraser. A prison officer sat outside the door.

Fraser said, 'You've got some news for me?' He was growing his beard again and it had just reached the stage where it was beginning to look like one.

'Yes,' said Tom. Agnes had difficulty in meeting his eyes.

'Important?'

'Yes,' Tom said again. He cleared his throat. 'In all our efforts to find out who killed Connie Flint, we rather lost sight of Dr Somersby. I include you in that — you seemed to forget about him as well.'

'How d'you mean?'

'You didn't ask Farleigh about his death at all, only about Connie's, even though Farleigh had a strong motive for killing Somersby.'

Fraser shrugged. 'Connie's was more important, the one I'd been accused of, the one I thought Leo guilty of. D'you know who killed him, then?'

'Yes.'

'Then, who?'

Tom said, 'When Somersby was killed, the only facts that the police had were that it was deliberate, and that it was done with a low-chassised car such as a sports car. You own a sports car, don't you?'

'Yes, I do, an MGB . . . ' Realisation crept into his face. 'You're not accusing *me*, are you?'

'No, I'm not saying you killed him . . . but that's not the same thing as saying your car wasn't used to do it.'

Fraser stared at him in disbelief. 'Are you saying it was my car?'

'No. Let's look at the other cars on the scene for a moment, Charles Flint's Merc, for instance.'

'Are you saying *he* did it?'

'I'm saying that his car did — but him? What's his motive? There are reasons he might want Connie dead, but Somersby?' He leaned forward. 'Who actually benefited from Somersby's death?'

'I suppose Leo and Ian, because John wouldn't take on the Alkovin trial.'

'I'd wondered about Terry Stroud, because Somersby wanted to get rid of him.'

'Yes, he did, didn't he?' Fraser said thoughtfully. 'Was it him?'

'There's someone we've both left out, someone else who benefited from Somersby's death.'

Fraser shrugged. 'I can only think of Connie herself, but she's . . . ' He looked from one to the other of them. 'D'you mean Connie?'

Tom slowly nodded.

'But how?'

'The first thing is that although this was a deliberate crime, it wasn't a premeditated one. Connie might have bitterly resented Somersby, but she hadn't seriously considered harming him.' He paused. 'But she did hate her husband, as you know. And with some reason, as *I* know — I've met him.'

'But what does that . . . ?'

'Connie's son, Sebi, had been staying with his father, but then, when Charles went on holiday with his girlfriend, Sebi went to stay with his mother. Now, Charlie dotes on his son, to the extent of letting him occasionally borrow his pride and joy, his car. He gave Sebi the keys before he left.

'But then Sebi fell ill, with flu. Connie nursed him, found the keys — and had an idea . . . Why not hit Charlie where it would really hurt him, in his surrogate scrotum. Steal his car and set fire to it.

'Sebi was delirious, we know that, although he does remember his mother giving him some pills. I think she gave him some sleeping pills. She drove to a garage to buy some paracetamol as cover, then went and took Charlie's car. Now, if you look on the map — ' Tom took one out and spread it on the table — 'you'll see that Charlie lived not so very far from Somersby, which is also the nearest lonely spot where she could set fire to the car and walk back to where she'd left her own.

'So she drives down the lane, here, and suddenly, there in front of her's the man who's spoiled her other chance at getting even with Charlie, not to mention making a name for herself — John Somersby . . . and on impulse, she hits him. Just a twitch of the wheel.'

'But then she ran over him again,' said Fraser. 'That must have been deliberate.'

'Yes, it was. Maybe she panicked, maybe it was in cold blood, we'll never know. But then, when she'd taken the car to where she had intended to fire it, she realised that it was hardly marked. She also realised that where a burnt-out car might be regarded suspiciously in Somersby's death, there would be no reason for the police to suspect Charlie's car. She, Connie, might be suspected, but not Charlie. So she drove it back to the garage, rubbed off what marks there were and left it.'

After a pause, Fraser said, 'Can you prove any of this?'

'Difficult, especially with Connie dead. But the exhaust pipe and other protruberances on the Merc match exactly with the injuries on Somersby's body, and Charles Flint does now remember some slight marks on the car when he returned. There was also a can of petrol in the back that he didn't put there. At the time, he assumed Sebi was responsible. The timing fits as well.'

Fraser paused while he absorbed this, then said, 'Do Sebi and Charles know?'

'Yes.'

'Poor Sebi.'

'Yes, poor Sebi. You have no difficulty in believing it yourself, then?'

'Not as I think about it, no. She *did* hate her husband, she told me. She was very eager, desperate almost, for some sort of professional achievement to hang up in front of him, and she did resent JS for not going with her over Alkovin.' He looked up at Tom. 'And she became unstable after that, irrational — not to mention the boozing . . . Aye, I can believe it.' He looked at Agnes, then back at Tom. 'But who killed her?'

Agne looked down at the table in front of her. Tom said, 'There we have another problem. Farleigh, as you have repeatedly told us, had both motive and opportunity — but he didn't do it — '

'That's what you say,' interrupted Fraser. 'How can you be so sure?'

'When people are in extremis, as Farleigh was under your attentions, you can usually tell when they're telling the truth.'

'That's subjective, to say the least.'

'So it is, but for now, you'll have to accept it. Moving on . . . Terry Stroud had a motive for killing Somersby, but not for killing Connie. Ian Saunders had a motive for killing Connie, but no opportunity. The same applies to Charlie.'

Fraser stared at him. 'You don't mean Sebi . . . '

'No.'

'For God's sake — who?'

'Frances.'

Fraser smiled and shook his head. 'Now you're being stupid.'

'Her fingerprints are on the stick that killed Connie, and also in Connie's hallway.'

'So what? She must have gone round there at some time.'

'Not so far as we can ascertain — Connie wasn't in the habit of inviting lab staff to her house. And there are microdots of Connie's blood on the clothes she was wearing that day. I'm sorry.'

'But her motive . . . ' He looked from one to the other of them. 'What motive could she have?'

'I phoned Dr Weisman in New York again, he probably being the world expert on the side-effects of Alkovin. He told me that it would be perfectly possible for someone who'd been on Alkovin for a while to commit an act of extreme violence *and then completely wipe it from their memory.* That's what Frances did. She has absolutely no idea of what she's done.'

'You — you can say that,' Fraser stuttered, 'b-but you got no proof an' I don' b-believe you . . . '

'Her car's been checked and there's gravel from Connie's drive in the tyres. And the timing fits exactly.'

'What timing?' Fraser said, although as he said it, he knew.

'She left your house at ten thirty. Connie rang you at ten forty and asked you to come round. Connie's house is on the route to Mary's — look . . . ' He pointed it out on the map.

'Frances, on a whim probably generated by the drug, decided to call on her, to plead your case with her perhaps — we'll never know. Whatever it was, it went wrong. Connie made Frances lose her temper, and you know what Frances was like at that stage when she lost her temper. Perhaps Connie said something detrimental to you, perhaps she tried to chuck her out. Whatever happened, Frances grabbed the stick in the hall, hit Connie with it and ran out, dropping it on the steps. She drove off and on the way to her mother's, somehow expunged it from her mind.' He looked at Fraser. 'She'd done that before on Alkovin, hadn't she? Wiped things out of her memory?'

Fraser reluctantly nodded and Tom continued:

'You, meanwhile, rang Mary and she told you that Frances was just arriving. You decided not to speak to her and went to Connie's where you found her body. The rest, you know.'

Agnes looked up, found his eyes and put her hands on his. 'I'm so sorry, Fraser.'

Fraser sat like stone.

'Does Mary know?' he said at last.

'Not yet,' Agnes said. 'She'll have to at some stage, though.'

Fraser opened his mouth, closed it, opened

318

it again, his lips twitching and trembling. 'Does Frances have to know?' he said at last.

'That,' said Tom, 'is the problem. I'm sorry to have to ask you this so bluntly, but is she going to survive?'

Fraser closed his eyes and compressed his lips . . . then he opened them and said, 'Probably not.'

'How long?'

'I've no idea, man — it could be months, it could even be a year . . . Whatever it is,' he beseeched them, 'she needs me. She can't know, *mustn't* know, but how am I going to get out of here if it doesn't come out . . . ?'

Agnes took over. 'We've been looking into it, Tom and Marcus and I. Marcus has high level contacts in the Home Office and we're as sure as we can be that we can get you out on bail.'

But Fraser had sunk his head into his hands and started crying.

Agnes said, 'Go, Tom — leave him to me. Please.'

Tom nodded, stood up and let his hand run over her shoulders as he passed behind her.

Outside, the prison officer said, 'You got a problem in there?'

'Yes,' Tom said. 'But it's better if you leave him with his solicitor for now.'